Selin's stories resemble video-clips in form and are just as visual, sparkling with maxims, aphoristic comparisons and witticisms. They are usually based on some fantastic plot involving fantastic metamorphoses happening to his characters and conveying Selin's wonder at life's inscrutable mysteries and inimitable beauty.

"Selin's stories are the finest in this collection of young writers..." — *Literary Gazette*

"Selin is a modern-day E.T.A. Hoffmann..." — *ExLibris*

Glas New Russian Writing

contemporary Russian literature

in English translation

Volume 31

Александр Селин, *Новый Романтик*

Alexander Selin

The New Romantic

Translated by Richard Cook

The Editors of the Glas series
Natasha Perova & Arch Tait & Joanne Turnbull

Front and back covers: *Fantasy in Brown* and
Diagonal Composition by Ruben Apresian

Camera-ready copy: Tatiana Shaposhnikova

GLAS Publishers
tel./tax: +7(095)441 9157
e-mail: perova@glas.msk.su

www.russianpress.com/glas
www.russianwriting.com

**As of 2002, Glas is distributed in North America by
NORTHWESTERN UNIVERSITY PRESS.**
Chicago Distribution Center, 11030 South Langley Avenue
Chicago, IL 60628, USA
tel: 1-800-621-2736 or 773-568-1550
fax: 1-800-621-8476 or 773-660-2235

ISBN 5-7172-0064-1

Printed at the Nauka printing press, Moscow

CONTENTS

Editors' Note

Alexander Selin belongs to that rare Chekhovian type of writer who tells a story not straightforwardly but through a series of carefully chosen and cleverly arranged vivid details. Perhaps Selin has even more in common with Gogol - he demonstrates the same kind of healthy humor and rich imagination.

At the same time he derives much of his literary merit from the absurdist writing of Daniil Kharms. Having said that it should be emphasized that Selin possesses a voice all his own and the three great writers mentioned above are only a point of reference.

Some of his stories resemble video-clips in form and are just as visual, sparkling with humor, aphoristic comparisons and wit. They are usually based on some fantastic plot involving fantastic metamorphoses happening to his characters and conveying Selin's wonder at life's inscrutable mysteries and inimitable beauty.

Selin grew up in the little town of Volzhsk on the Volga. He graduated from the Moscow Institute of Physics Engineering and worked as a physicist for eight years, leaving this profession with a number of publications and discoveries to his credit. During that time he wrote prose and plays, which he staged himself with theatre companies in Moscow and St Petersburg. He also writes film and TV scripts and humorous short stories, published in literary journals and recited by comic actors.

He has two collections of short stories and the novel *Videountermenschen* to his name.

Translator's Note

Critics were at a loss to find a category into which Selin's work, full of wit and inventiveness, can be slotted. Gogol and Kharms were mentioned as influences, but not with any certainty. Finally they concluded that Selin is Selin and really his own man. That is good enough for me. Selin graduated in Engineering Physics before becoming a writer. This helps me to confess that this translator graduated as a dentist before becoming a translator/writer. We are both in a sense, playing away from home, and for my part I feel absolved by this from making any attempt at exegetical analysis or ranking of the author within the Russian literary canon. It is probably too early for that anyway, though no doubt somebody somewhere is doing just that.

For my part, I have been driven by sheer enjoyment and continuing curiosity. The themes are the usual suspects: Love, Death, Affliction, Fear, Obsession. But the treatments can be variable. I rapidly became accustomed to his avoidance of the neat ending or twist in the tail. Selin is not for those who want in music "a tune they can whistle" or a signalled coda to finish with, in art they want a picture "that tells a story", and in literature a simple narrative with a beginning, a middle and an end. We are sometimes left in the air, but somehow satisfied.

"The Parachutist" takes us into magic realism of a sort. Magical realist Salman Rushdie's "Satanic Verses" opens with the free fall of his main characters from an airliner over the English Channel, who survive the event. The parachutist Lacis is accompanied in his free fall by "Death", a woman who appears subsequently in a whole wardrobe of disguises, but who operates in an utterly naturalistic world. Remembering how "The Devil" walks the earth in *The Master and Margarita* we can now add Bulgakov to our tally of influences. Selin's "Death" character is often a skittish female who dresses unstylishly, hitch-hikes and takes tea without sugar. She evolves literally into a "femme fatale", while somehow remaining a simpering, tearful Mills and Boon character. Like all of the females represented she is a pre-feminism caricature.

"The Sniper" is an essay in fear and human frailty. The sniper never actually shoots anybody, but the sense of his menace remains with us after the narrative ends. It left me chillingly conscious of the ambivalent attitude that has always existed between society and its protectors. This message will not be lost on the inhabitants of Washington DC.

"Lolita" tests us similarly. Is she real, or an idealized counterpoint to her husband's squalid sexual exploits? Does she play echo to Nabokov's eponymous nymphet?

In Selin's stories wives can suffer casual physical abuse at the hands of their menfolk. Is this, as the Sotsrealist might argue, typical? The caricaturing seems to be intentional. Selin is a very visual writer. We are offered telling images rather than character analysis. The casual abuse which the wives in "Billy Goat" and "Itching" suffer may not be either stereotypical or realistic, but merely represent an indifference to actuality if it should interfere with the author's pre-occupation with visual presentation.

Magic is also present in "Sablin and Sologub". The characters here live in a world of constant duelling, in which even a surgeon's profession takes second place to it, a world where the surgeon's powers include control of the speed and direction of his opponents' bullets.

Most hilarious for me is "Alpatovka". This is a village where every inhabitant is a liar and a thief, where every described object has been, is being, or will be stolen. Blame for this exuberant criminality is burdened upon the legendary surrounding forest, eternally voracious. The writing is sheer joy. I can't find and don't want a label for it.

But these are sample thoughts. My pre-occupation has been with seeking an authentic English analogue for this extraordinary man's writing. The necessary immersion in it has left me too close to the texts to have any objectivity about it. Selin seems to tell us: "This is the Selin world. Nobody else's. Read it or not." Reading it has given me such huge pleasure that I will merely add a heartfelt: "And enjoy the fun!"

Richard Cook

The Parachutist

The veteran world-class parachutist Edvardas Lacis was doing one of his famous free-fall jumps.

The customary delight he felt over the free-fall pirouettes, practised during the twelve thousand jumps of his career, turned to alarm when the time came to pull the ripcord. It refused to give. These things happened in his richly filled life. The thing to do was to stay sufficiently calm and try again. Lacis tugged at the D-ring again with such force that it made him spin like a top in the air current. The parachute didn't open. Once more he tried. Again nothing. The prospect of a free-fall touchdown swam vividly into his mind.

"I'm really in it now!" Lacis wheezed, trying to will the earth out of sight with his eyes. With a final effort of concentration he tugged at the ring with his petrified hands for the last time. The ring ripped off and flew up into the air, gathering speed for its own descent. And the parachute... it stayed as unfurled as if it had never existed.

A true veteran meets his death calmly. But even now Edvardas had enough sang-froid to notice that someone was flying at his side.

It surely couldn't be Gorbunov, the next in line, catching up. No it wasn't. Not Gorbunov by his side, but a female form...

It was Death. Skinny, in a fluttering shapeless gown, which she kept adjusting as a windbreak to keep on the same level as the doomed parachutist.

"Let's have your last wish then, sharpish!" yelled Death, trying to make herself heard over the roar and hiss of the air currents. "Go on. D'you hear? Quick!"

Lacis kept quiet, thoroughly petrified.

"I'm not offering you a glass of vodka and a quick drag," Death yelled. "You won't hold them at this speed. Maybe you want to leave money to your relatives, eh? Take revenge on the chute-packers maybe?"

Lacis didn't answer.

"So what's up? Swallowed your tongue in fright, have you? Come on, let's have it, you mother you! You're going to crash in a minute. Think quickly, you dimwit!"

Lacis kept silent, transfixed by the sight of the green fields and network of country lanes hurtling towards him.

"Come on. Anything you like. Must I do your

thinking for you? Come on. Time's short! I'm counting to three: one, two, two and a half... Three!"

"A spare parachute," Lacis babbled. (It was the only thing on his mind).

Death was surprised, but all the same, nodded.

Lacis was immediately tossed upwards: the usual state the parachutist experiences when the canopy opens, and from somewhere down below came the sound of an ambulance siren and cries of despair.

The parachute had opened at a dangerously low height and the soles of his feet hit the ground painfully even though he had carefully bent his knees in good time. He didn't unstrap his harness, and, pulled by the wind, he was dragged across the grass for a long time. He simply paid no attention to this trivial matter. He was stiff, he was stunned, he had survived.

Then hands were pulling at him. Here they were; his team mates, instructors, colonels, doctors running towards him. "Edvardas, Ed. He's alive!" as if from a far, far distant radio.

Within ten minutes they had Lacis heading for town in the station minibus. During that time he uttered not a single word, and gave not a single reply to any question.

"Lost the power of speech, have we?" asked the instructor.

Lacis shook his head and continued to gaze at the flat countryside as it raced past. Everything was like being in an adolescent dream, when you fall down, cry out, and suddenly wake up. Then after all this, you find you're not in bed but in a bus... "Must be some sort of delirium," thought Lacis, waving his hand as if to ward off some pestering insect, and rubbing his temples. He looked out of the window and gasped. At the roadside stood a familiar lean figure, whom he had only seen out of the corner of his eye for several seconds but who he would never forget. At the road edge stood Death. No longer in the shapeless flowing gown, but in army fatigues. Her head was twirling around in dismay. With one hand she was scratching her neck and with the other thumbing a lift.

"Step on it!" bawled Lacis.

"Ah you're back in the land of the living, are you?" The instructor was overjoyed. "You're OK. What's the point? We could pick the fellow up. It's about three kilometres to town. It seems a bit mean. Let's go back and get him."

"No, let's get home quick. I'm not feeling too grand..."

"We could still pick him up, eh?"

"No!"

Lacis scarcely greeted his wife when they arrived. He fell on to the divan and with unblinking eyes, stared at the cracks in the ceiling plaster.

"Would you like a bite to eat?" Valentina didn't

wait for a reply but got busy at the stove, accustomed to his taciturnity. She only roused him after an insistent ringing of the telephone.

"Take the phone, Lacis. It's Gorbunov. Don't shrink away from me! Wake up! It's Gorbunov."

Although you could say that Gorbunov was Lacis' best friend, they were emotionally and temperamentally at opposite poles. He was forever laughing, and even though he was of a respectable age (they were both well into their thirties) he had a ruddy complexion.

"You had us all in a sweat!" laughed Gorbunov. "I jumped after you, then you disappeared from view. I thought all sorts of things. What iron nerves you have, old man! Ha-ha!"

"I'm tired, Sergei." Edvardas was trying to end the conversation without offending Gorbunov.

"I understand, I really do," again he burst into laughter... "Yes, you would be, ha-ha-ha! Really! Where did you get that parachute, black with red stripes? Imported I bet, eh?"

"Yes, imported."

"I've got it, if you... I picked it up. Otherwise mind, you'd forget. I'll say thank you, I'll jump with it myself."

"No. Don't. Really Sergei..." Lacis broke into a cough. "Really. Look, bury it somewhere... you don't understand? How can I make it clear? OK, I'll bury it myself. Yes, yes, thanks, thanks. I'm having a sleep now."

Edvardas dreamt about exactly what had been on

his mind as he fell asleep, about his applying for early retirement because... that was the most difficult part, to produce a plausible and inoffensive reason for cutting himself off from that congenial group of parachutists, with which he was deeply bonded and which in spite of his general taciturnity, he very much loved. He even dreamt about the farewell banquet in his honour. A ceremonial speech by Gorbunov rich in parachutist anecdotes. Then a presentation from his friends, a memorial album of photographs. Finally and most important, an oil painting picturing Lacis touching down on a spare parachute, black with red stripes. At this point he woke up.

"Get up. Someone to see you." Valentina was shaking him.

Edvardas yawned and dragged himself into the hallway. In the doorway stood Death, looking very imposing and intellectual, dressed in a long coat and hat. Under the coat a suit and a white shirt with a tie.

"Sorry to come so late in the day." Death lowered her gaze. "I won't keep you long."

"Come in," said Lacis as if programmed, and led Death into the room.

"Would you like some tea?"

"Thank you. I won't refuse."

Death having adjusted her tie perched on the edge of the chair.

"No sugar please."

"Valya," he called, "some tea please."

"Maybe a spot of supper?"

"Thank you, I've eaten my fill." Death looked around the room with curiosity, sipping tea from the newly arrived tea-glass.

"I've come about a certain matter, Edvardas Lacis."

"You seem well-acquainted with my name?"

"Well, rather! Information comes with the job. Bloody hell... What a stupid cock-up... Hell!"

Lacis just sat, neither alive nor dead, dishevelled and crumpled from his half-sleep.

"You needn't pinch yourself, Lacis, it's not a dream... What a cock-up it turned out to be. Bloody hell!"

"What cock-up?" babbled the parachutist.

"You remember, Lacis," said Death. "I saved your life."

Lacis began to fiddle about, toss about, stumbling into expressions of gratitude, getting his turns of speech mixed up, cases and gerunds.

"Let me fetch a spot of cognac," he somehow concluded unconvincingly.

"Not worth it. I won't be here long, and I don't drink, well only in the odd moment of weakness. I want you to understand, Lacis, that your survival is a mistake, at someone else's expense. Jesus, what sort of blackout was that with the parachute? A few seconds to think! I just didn't put my thoughts together. Like an automaton

I granted your wish. First time ever, really, such embarrassment. I've had a lot of experience with parachutists in a similar situation. Usually they either yell obscenities, or ask to kiss their wives, but it never occurred to anyone to ask for a spare parachute. And me? I must have been in a kind of trance and I was just stupid, and it bloody opened. Bloody Hell!"

"Yes, yes, thank you, thank you." Lacis was now wide awake.

"I understand you have an obligation; it's your job, but yes, if that's what happened... Thank you enormously, I'm much obliged, and how can I thank you? Perhaps a nip of cognac all the same?"

"No. Though... No-no. Obliged, you say?"

"Yes-yes."

"Well, Lacis, now we're talking business. You understand, we have these rules... and you are as it were, registered with me. But since it's my own fault I grant you a year, at most a year and a half..."

"What do you mean, a year and a half?"

"You can live on about a year and a half, but then you are on your honour to go back."

"Where?"

"What do you mean, where? There, where I fished you out this morning. What a scatterbrain I was... that bloody parachute..."

Lacis took the point and his face went pale.

"But I'm only thirty five."

"So what, thirty-five? It's a good age, not a child. That you could call a tragic age to die. Twenty's not really interesting — a youngster dying a foolish death. Seventy-five — well that sort of speaks for itself, a commonplace sort of death. But thirty-five — that's, well... Eh, don't undervalue your age, Lacis. At such an age you understand, you start to have an intelligent awareness of mortality. Then you stay long in people's memories. Your friends respect you. Don't undervalue your age, Lacis. Did you ever do jumps with Kondukov?"

"No. He was with another garrison."

"Yes, he was from another garrison, but you see, you remember Kondukov because Artem Kondukov turned up at thirty-four and not at seventy-five. A great guy Kondukov. He managed in those fatal seconds before Wham! he crashed into a sheep pen, to tell me to get stuffed. Unsentimental. A real man! All right then, Lacis. Two years. Not a day over. God I hate this haggling!"

"But why should this have to happen?" Edvardas was becoming agitated.

"I love life. I love my wife... Why? There are people... who want to die. So many get mown down in wars. It matters little to you. And I, well I'm studying English."

"So what? I'm also studying."

"I'm booked for a tour abroad."

"So? Go on your tour. Neither interferes."

"I'm much obliged. I understand... But I beg you

since you've saved me once be generous once more. Let me live my life out. Let me die a natural death."

Death smirked.

"And I'll pray to God for you. I won't do another stupid thing. I promise."

"That's enough, Lacis, you're not in a monastery and I'm not your priest. 'Pray to God', 'Not one sin more'. You could have said 'I'll kill two others instead of me' then I'd think about it. Who wants your 'pray to God'? What sort of helpmate is he? So how about killing two others? Or one?"

Lacis again paled, shook his head.

"Well, I never! Now watch out or I won't even give you twenty-four hours. You'll snuff it tomorrow. I'm going to count to three. One! Two! Two and a half... You still refuse?"

Lacis was silent.

"Three! My patience is exhausted. Now take care, my ungrateful Baltic friend." Death quickly moved off into the hallway and put on hat and coat. "And I've been offering him another two years to live! So long. Oh and by the way when's your next jump?"

"Never. I'm retiring."

"Ah, so that's it, he's retiring... So retire, clever dick then, retire! Carry on, but on this earth, brother, Death is on the watch no less than in the sky and it wouldn't be as honourable, believe me... One such stubborn chap died on me by choking in the bath after a booze-up, instead of going heroically in a burning tank. And also pick up that parachute of mine from Gorbunov and return it. It's mine after all."

"Yes, of course. Where shall I bring it?"

"I'll ring you and we'll fix a time and place. I'll think about it. Good night. Mark the time. Less than twenty-four hours, you understand? Regards to your wife and the team. I won't say goodbye. Au revoir."

Death went out, banging the door.

For the first time in his life Lacis locked the door with all three locks, flopped on to the divan, and fell asleep immediately.

"Who was that who came last night?" Valentina asked in the morning.

"Just an acquaintance," groaned Edvardas, now understanding that he really hadn't been dreaming it all.

"So elegant and polite."

"Oh yes, polite."

"Are you having a bath?"

"On no account."

Lacis suddenly remembered the parachute and rang Gorbunov who promised to bring it round within the hour.

Lacis had decided not to let Gorbunov in on his problems, knowing the unselfish recklessness his friend was capable of in time of danger.

He simply took the parachute and mentioned his firm decision about retiring.

Gorbunov sat for a long time head in hands.

"You say your nerves are shattered."

"Yes Sergei, and there's something not right in general with my health. And in our job, you yourself know, that if you have doubts, it's better to go in good time."

"Go in good time you say? Are you a footballer to think of finishing at thirty-five? In our business at thirty-five dawn's just breaking."

"That's right, Sergei. But on the other hand, at thirty-five you get this intelligent awareness of mortality, your friends respect you, you remain long in peoples' memories," Lacis broke into a cough.

"That doesn't sound like you, Ed." Gorbunov looked straight into Lacis' eyes. "Not your style! Oh dear, someone's been getting at you..." Gorbunov turned towards the kitchen where as before Valentina was busying herself, grinned and switched to whispering, "Don't listen to women I'm telling you. Their main interest is to keep you captive, at home. It's women, I tell you, women that'll be the end of you. Not parachute jumps."

Edvardas shivered.

"As far as I'm concerned, it's better to finish a long career smashed to pieces than to die, curled up on an ottoman. Not now of course, but at some age like seventy-odd. I want to spit on death the skinny stupid sod."

"Shh! Quiet!"

"In short, don't play the fool," Gorbunov began to speak deliberately loudly. "That's between ourselves of course, Ed, you must have heard about the tournament in Krakow. They want to include us both in the national team again."

"Is that true?" Valentina emerged from the kitchen.

"You heard me? Yes, my love," Gorbunov grabbed Valentina by the waist and lifted her. "What a great husband you've got. The acrobat of free fall. The king of perfect jumps. Ha-ha-ha!"

"Good for you, lads!" Valentina smiled.

"That's it then, squire," Gorbunov winked at Lacis. "We're carrying on jumping. It's settled. You'll see me to the bus-stop?"

"Sure," Lacis looked sadly at his watch, remembering Death's promise to sort things out with him within 24 hours, and stood up to take his friend to the bus stop.

Walking back, the angry roar of a revving up engine made him suddenly turn. From round the corner burst a lorry and without signalling, roared at full speed towards Lacis. The smirk on the driver's face seemed familiar, even seen through the dirty windscreen. Lacis gasped, and with a couple of steps, flung himself into a trimmed bush next to the roadside lawn.

The lorry, without slackening speed raced on and gouged into the rear bodywork of a mini, parked at the roadside.

"I'll twist your block off!" shouted the car owner brandishing a crowbar and charging after the lorry, without success. With broad springing bounces the lorry driver shot away, abandoning his lorry, and disappeared from view. The upset mini owner shuffled back to inspect the damage.

"Did you manage to see who it was?" The driver approached Lacis who was crawling out of the bushes."

"I think so. That's to say, No."

"Me too. I never got a good look at him. Skinny, lanky, quick. If I catch him I'll kill him! Did you see the car number? So, no number! Just a "Driving School" sign. That's how they teach them now! He almost killed you, and look what he's done to my car, the bastard."

Lacis nodded in sympathy, and pushing through the gawping crowd set off home with firm strides, glancing all around him. He had just turned the corner of his five-storey apartment block when he turned green. Leaning her back against the brick wainscot stood Death who gave a heavy sigh.

"Where is he now?"

"Who?"

"That twit with the crowbar?"

"He's there with his car."

"What an idiot he is. He's roused the whole neighbourhood with that crowbar. You see, Lacis, the citizenry doesn't absorb culture too well. All right, there was an accident and I am guilty. But we might have been able to settle the matter peaceably. Now the whole street is out. Well, have a look round the corner for me. Have they dispersed yet?"

Lacis looked.

"No."

"Never mind. Carry on; my business just now isn't with you. I've got to get that lorry away."

Lacis timidly moved off but with an effort of will made himself stop and turn round.

"Excuse me. Was that lorry supposed to kill me?"

"No, not really," Death smiled. "No. If I really had that in mind you can be sure I'd have done it. I just took a drive. Generally speaking, the traffic accident method is unreliable. Not worth using. A lot of noise and as you see, it doesn't work. Where was I, oh hell? Off you go then. Live out your time. The promised hours are coming to an end. Enjoy them. Your wife's frying mushrooms. I can smell them from here. What a smell!"

Getting home, Lacis threw the mushrooms right from the frying pan into the rubbish bucket.

"Don't buy on the street corner," he growled at the astonished Valentina.

"I didn't. I got them in the shop."

"All the same, don't buy them any more!"

"Then what should I buy?" Valentina got angry. "You pick them up and chuck them out. You've always eaten mushrooms. What's this lunacy, Lacis? Yesterday a strange parachute arrives, now your face is all scratched.

It's the second day you've not been yourself. What's happened? Let me in on it."

Lacis embraced Valentina and looked gloomily at the wall clock.

"I'll try to explain. Give me a little time."

Lacis sat pensive for a long time staring at the second hand on the clock-face, which, with carefree stupid joy, completed, one after another its repulsive circles. Then he switched his attention to the minute hand which moved significantly slower, but moved no less meanly, covering the divisions on the dial with enviable doggedness.

The hour hand was as if motionless. But it was only seemingly still. You had to close your eyes and get distracted, then after a while open them, and this, utterly serene hand, taking advantage of your distraction would jump forward so that you shuddered, as millions of people shudder who are late for work or for the train, as lovers who have missed a date or their wedding, or as surgeons in the emergency ward shudder, together with the relatives of a hopeless case.

"Stop, Time! Keep still you hour hand!" But it keeps on moving.

"How time flies!" muttered Lacis.

"You what?"

"I was saying, Valya, that time flies." He embraced his wife. "Do you remember the day we first met?"

Just then the telephone rang.

"It was a clear day and you had a pink dress on and some funny plaits which stuck up."

The telephone rang again.

Lacis breathed heavily.

"Don't pick it up, Valya. Where were we? Yes, when we met you were wearing a pink dress. And then I tried straight away to see you home, but I clumsily dropped my ice-cream..."

The telephone didn't stop.

"I went up to the fountain to clean my trousers, but you wouldn't wait and ran off..."

"I'll have to pick it up all the same."

"I'm not in."

Valentina took the phone.

"He's not in."

"I was so upset then and I thought I'd never see you again. I wasn't myself for a whole week. Several times a day I went up to that fountain and looked all around to see if I could spot a pink dress."

There was a hammering on the door.

"Then I recognized you in the crowd by your pink dress and your plaits."

The angry fist drumming on the door continued wildly.

"Don't open it, Valentina... Then I understood it wasn't just the matter of a pink dress..."

It was obvious that now feet were being used on the door. Lacis broke into a sweat.

"So then we ate some ice-cream together. And then I accompanied you for the second time. We said goodbye and I asked for a kiss. You ran off again. I was ashamed. Again I wasn't myself the whole week and I went several times a day to the fountain to see if I could spot a pink dress..."

At that moment the knocking suddenly stopped.

"Lord, they surely haven't given up," marvelled Lacis, looking at his watch. The twenty-four hour threat of yesterday had run its course. "It can't be!" And flushing, he flopped into the armchair.

"What nice things you've been saying, Edvardas," said Valentina in a trembling voice.

Just then there came from the street a piercing whistle immediately followed by a cobblestone crashing through the sitting room window.

Edvardas went out on to the balcony.

"Stop playing silly buggers. It's OK by me but you could have hit my wife!"

"Then don't get her to lie and say you're out!" shouted Death, adjusting her cap and stuffing her hands into her pockets.

"Why are you hanging about then? Come out into the street!"

"No, I'm not coming out."

"So!" Death lit a cigarette to give herself time to concentrate. "So. And where's the parachute, my parachute? Get after it, sharpish."

"Take it then!" Lacis flung the parachute from the balcony. "Take it and get lost. Stay out of my sight!"

"What's this? Getting a sharp tongue now, are we? I let you survive for twenty-four hours. Time to say your last farewells."

"You let me survive? Learn to drive a lorry first, you stupid bag of bones. Sod off!"

"Well, well... How he's beginning to talk! Who are you calling a bag of bones, you shit? Your saviour? You're living on borrowed time, understand?"

"It's you that's living on borrowed time, that's who!"

At that point Valentina came out on to the balcony.

"Don't mess with hooligans, Edvardas. Come inside. You've just been saying such nice things to me."

Edvardas returned to the sitting room.

After about ten minutes he pulled himself together with some difficulty and completed the monologue he had begun.

From that day on, Valentina exulted in her husband's meticulousness and, as it seemed to her, excessive conscientiousness.

He put a spy-hole in the door, and shut off the balcony with latches. He was extraordinarily cautious when dealing with electrical appliances and the gas stove. He stopped drinking spirits and took showers instead of baths.

"Better for you. Stimulating," he would smile at his wife.

He always took the underground passageways when crossing the street.

"I reckon the true Balt in you is coming out," Valentina remarked. She liked the changes in her husband's behaviour. "You've become precise and self-disciplined like all true Balts."

"You see," pondered Lacis, "the land of my forebears, Latvia, was constantly in some sort of danger from a multitude of causes. This conditioned the people to respect punctuality and order. What's more, we were aware of this danger every day. Not only in the air but also on land and at sea. Did you know that Letts mustn't even relax in the bath?"

"Why is that?" Valentina was surprised.

"You see the splashing warm water in the bath dulls the native vigilance of the Lett, so he could relax and choke, especially if drunk, and that's why he drinks in moderation."

He wasn't allowed to transfer to the reserve. Gorbunov himself tore up the application saying to his chief: "It'll pass, I know," and persuaded them to grant him leave "to think it over" and come to his senses. And he also took leave himself, out of solidarity with his friend.

Both couples decided to holiday together as usual in the Crimea, in the army holiday home.

The sea is always so bracing. Especially for people from Central Russia, wearied by the heavy torpor of the city in summer. The change of climate and the salt content of the sea water heal better than time, blunting the ache of emotional wounds and onerous memory.

Those, travelling to resorts in the south, are not usually conscious of the reason why. Afterwards, they report back in the form of browned bodies, photographs against palm trees, and amateur seaside souvenirs. No super-specialist on a high-level mission ever compiles a report with such care and precision, from the minute of arrival, as a holiday-maker, who is gathering evidence about his stay at a seaside resort. This is so that for the next few months he can demonstrate to himself and to others that he was really there, that it was great, and, "Oh how unfortunate that you weren't there with us!"

My advice is: don't get sunburnt on the beach, don't take photos or collect souvenirs and you will have a genuinely good vacation; and keep your summer impressions to yourself, when your work colleagues ask, "How was it in the Crimea?" you reply, "What Crimea? We spent the whole summer in the countryside near Moscow." At least they'll leave you alone after that.

For the first time in his life, Edvardas Lacis was having a proper rest at a seaside resort. Because now, accepted values meant little to him. And so the change of climate and landscape slowly but surely exerted their healing effect. And taking into account the fact that the cutter he had been out in three times had not capsized, the sight-seeing bus had not overturned, and not once had he been poisoned by the food, so in place of anxiety there gradually developed a state of vital optimism.

Once, it is true, he was walking in the hills towards evening when a boulder from up the hill thundered down and crashed within a couple of metres of him. Edvardas for a long time inspected the slope and the summit but could not see anybody who could have done it.

He dreamt one and the same dream every night, but it was getting more optimistic and colourful every night. Violet shades would alternate with light blue ones. That overcast sky which had obtained during that memorable jump was now more and more filled with sunlight. Already even that black spare parachute didn't seem so sombre. And Death herself was all affability and kindness.

In the dream he would see himself as a detached third party. And the dream would be in slow motion. There would be the D-ring flying off into space. Death would appear in those shapeless flowing garments. Then they are in close-up. Both are laughing and having an animated conversation. Death slaps him on the shoulder in a friendly manner. And at that perilously low altitude the black parachute opens. Lacis stretches out his legs and touches the grass, bends his knees, spreads his arms for balance. Or rather he throws his arms up victoriously. Gestures of approval from the instructor. Then of course the fans come running, laden with flowers. Edvardas is smiling as he is being dragged behind the canopy inflated by the gusty wind. He doesn't unfasten the straps. He doesn't do this on purpose. He simply doesn't want to take them off, which is, in fact, contrary to instructions.

"Did you have a good dream?" asks Valentina.

"Yes, Valya. I've just had a lovely dream."

The seaside resort was certainly improving his health. Both couples enjoyed their vacation, laughing a lot as in previous stays here, and generally gave no thought to unhappy memories. Even Edvardas seemed in no hurry about his resolve to quit parachute sport. All the recent unpleasantness seemed now rather distant, and even more, over for good. This seemed more apparent with every new untroubled seaside day.

Sunshine, fresh air, regular meals and trips in the cutter... guitar music in the evenings... And also the jokes and yarns spun by Gorbunov with take-offs of parachute acrobatic skills on the drop-zone of the hotel bedroom floor.

Lacis still avoided the mud baths but he'd now join the others for a drink. And why not, when you're on vacation, and not just anywhere but in the Crimea, with the guitar playing and jokes exchanged in the company of friends.

"Hello, you've got badly burned, mate." Gorbunov accidentally came across Lacis who had dropped off on the open beach. "After those two bottles of the strong stuff you should have got under the umbrella. Otherwise you burn. And spirits make it worse. You're usually more careful!"

As is well-known anti-sunburn cream doesn't really help, and in the evening Lacis' temperature shot up. Gorbunov tried several folk remedies he had been assured were effective. He poured beer on his friend's back and tried some other stuff, but nothing worked. He then suggested urinating on Lacis' inflamed skin, which Lacis refused.

"All right then. Call the doctor. If he recommends it then you can piss on me!"

Gorbunov dashed down to the ground floor to seek out some sort of doctor. He was gone a long time but finally returned with a skinny doctor, like a beanpole in a white coat and dark glasses.

"Lie down on your stomach, patient!" the doctor commanded, the moment he came into the room. "And take your vest off."

Then he sat at the patient's side and began to probe with his fingers over the sunburnt back, looking now at the patient and now at Gorbunov who was still in the room.

"What cold hands you have, doctor!" said Edvardas, pulling away.

"It's not my hands that are cold but your back that is hot," said the doctor with a nasal whine. He became pensive, biting his lip, and then asked Gorbunov to leave him alone with the patient.

"He won't croak, will he?" laughed Gorbunov as he left the room.

"Stop making jokes like that," the doctor cut in. "Death is not at all a laughing matter!" Then he turned back to the patient. "How old are you, patient?"

"Thirty five. Why?"

"No matter. A good age."

The doctor stood up and shut the door on the latch. He probed the vertebral column along its whole length once more.

"So what's going on?" Lacis was getting tired of the doctor's vagueness.

"Your case is very serious, my friend." The doctor had moved into familiar tone and whispered tenderly. "We'll need to operate."

"What is there to operate about?" Lacis sat up.

"Lie down!"

"Look, all that's wrong with me is sunburn!"

"And I'm telling you to lie down and don't turn round." The doctor swiftly opened his instrument bag and began fiddling inside with the surgical metalware. "So many of them here," he whispered nasally. "How many different things there are!"

It seemed he was lost in the sheer variety of ringing metalware.

"No, this won't do, too short. Ah! Here it is!" Finally he had a long scalpel shining in his hand.

"There's something I don't understand. You must

be joking! What d'you mean operate?" Lacis obediently didn't raise his head but he tensed up all over. "Why operate? You plan to do it right here?"

"Where else? Certainly not on the beach. Why put it off? We've been putting it off long enough. I mean the disease must not be neglected."

"What disease are you talking about? Have you got me mixed up with somebody else, doctor?"

"No, no mistake."

"Now all I've got is a bad sunburn. Are you going to remove my skin? I don't understand!"

"Don't turn round!" shrieked the doctor.

However Lacis noticed that the doctor was gripping the scalpel not in a pen-grip but in his fist. Lacis jumped up and sat on the ottoman. He was getting frightened.

"Stay where you are! Lie down this minute." The doctor approached him confidently.

"We've disturbed you for nothing, doctor." Edvardas was trembling all over, "It would be better to let Gorbunov urinate on my back."

"He can do that later. You called the doctor, so I'm simply not going away."

"I refuse!"

"So you're against our national health care? Be careful what you say!" the doctor hissed and, brandishing the scalpel, flung himself at the parachutist.

Edvardas instinctively shielded himself with the

pillow, and the scalpel with a whistle cutting through the air ripped into the pillow, releasing feathers which flew all over the room. Lacis pushed the doctor with the torn pillow and flung himself at the door, forgetting it was on the latch.

The doctor, while trying to spit out his mouthful of feathers, was preparing for another attempt to operate on his patient. In his other hand appeared some kind of surgical saw.

Edvardas bent down and tugged at the carpet, making the doctor lose his balance and fall on the floor. Jumping over him Lacis took two more steps and jumped off the balcony. Fortunately he had judged the height well, knowing that he had been only on the second floor. His feet painfully struck the asphalt, but he softened the fall by pulling himself together rapidly and rolled away from the landing place. Quite close he heard the clink of a scalpel striking the road. Not wishing to stick around as the surgical saw sang through the air, Edvardas jumped up and made off.

"He's gone off, the reptile. Never mind. I'll get you on the operating table yet!" yelled the doctor, among other things that Lacis couldn't make out.

He flew on regardless through bushes, jumping over benches and terrifying holidaymakers. Leaving the tourist area he found a deserted spot near the water and crouched behind a boulder to be out of sight. Then he carefully scanned the semi-deserted evening beach. He observed no signs of pursuit. Some distance away he could hear a trio of lifeguards sharing a bottle. The portable *shashlik* stall was still doing business. Its bearded proprietor was dressed in a white overall and wearing dark glasses. Lacis watched him for a while, about maybe three minutes, but none of his activities seemed at all suspicious.

"Oh hell!" Edvardas spat into a rising wave. "What's been going on? Was it a doctor who came to see me or who?" Then he despairingly shouted at the sea: "So I have to be forever on the run now?"

He was staring at the sea as if there were some hope there, as if waiting for a reply. The squawking seagulls were flying low. Somewhere in the distance a coastguard cutter was patrolling... and then in the rosy sunlit track from the horizon, the pipe of a scuba diver appeared above the surface. Lacis half rose and then, enfeebled, sat down again. The pipe came directly at him with no deviation or zig-zags. He could see the gentle breakers from the diver's moving frame. Lacis paled. He heard the flippers plop on the water several times. "How fast he's going!" Lacis muttered to himself, "unnaturally fast." At that moment a trident from a sporting gun rose above the surface.

"This is it!" Edvardas hid himself and convulsively clutched a handful of pebbles.

By then the masked face of the swimmer had risen above the water. A final flourish from the flippers and the swimmer rose out of the water. He approached. The wet mask made it difficult to examine his features. Lacis' mouth turned dry...

Gorbunov pulled off the mask and snorting like a walrus came out of the water. "Look who's here! What are you sitting there for? The water's really nice. Why don't you have a swim?"

And with great pride he pulled out a medium-size fish from his trunks, the only trophy of his underwater hunting.

Late that night they were returning together from the local cinema. They continued to discuss what had taken place with the doctor several hours previously.

"I don't understand anything. I specially went again to the medical station, and they said there had never been any doctor with a goatee and dark glasses. What a son of a bitch!"

"So where did you find him, Sergei, for goodness sake?"

"Well, I didn't search specially," Gorbunov looked down, "he sort of found me. The medical station was closed for a supper break, and this guy in a white coat came up to me. 'What,' he says, 'sick then, are we?' 'No, not me,' I say. 'It's my friend!' 'And who's this friend of yours?' he asks and takes out his notepad. 'Edvardas Lacis,' I say, 'Room 36. He's got a bad sunburn. He's a parachutist.' This guy jumps up, unlocks the office, picks up his bag and follows me." ˙

"Did you get a good look at his face?" Lacis shuddered.

"Sort of. Skinny, pallid as I remember, goatee and dark glasses. Doctors all look the same to me in their white coats... What do you mean?"

"Yes, probably a false beard, and glasses to distract attention." Edvardas looked gloomy. "And his voice, sort of put on, not genuine..."

"Yes, a real shit, eh!" Gorbunov spat viciously. "But how could I know that such nutters could be about in a place like this? Your back improving then, by the way?"

"Yes, I hardly think about it now."

"Well, you see, we have one good result at least. Maybe it could become a new method of psychotherapy?" Gorbunov laughed heartily.

"Oh get off with you. Enough! But certainly no more sunbathing."

They turned into a side alley winding through fragrant acacias. On either side stood plaster statues and in the distance the box-like buildings of the holiday hotel. It was still a long walk. While Lacis remained silent and morose, Gorbunov's attention turned to one of the plaster figures.

"Looks like a ballerina you think?"

"Looks like it."

"And that one with a pick in his hand. A geologist you reckon?"

"Yes, a geologist. With no ears."

"And this one?"

"Must be a doctor," he went on in disgust, "with no nose."

"There must have been a nose. Been knocked off! You know, Lacis, I understand that these sculptures are considered tasteless these days, but on the other hand there is in them some sort of meaning for us now."

"What sort of meaning?"

"This. A man's walking along this alley. Let's say a footballer. And there you are! He sees a sculpture of a footballer. He thinks, 'Look, somebody has thought it worthwhile to immortalize my work, and I'm content to play in a half-hearted way.' He will feel ashamed and he will begin to score more goals. What's up with you?"

Lacis stood as if rooted to the ground. The next statue was of a parachutist at the moment of landing. Arms spread wide. Knees bent. Straps across the chest. And a cone of rods rearing from the rucksack depicting, evidently, the stretched rigging lines.

"Damn it!" Lacis froze.

The acacia branches rustled sorrowfully. The moon gave the sculpted surface a greenish tinge.

Gorbunov was frankly overjoyed.

"Look at that, they haven't forgotten our profession either! You know it makes me want to jump right now, honestly. It may not be a great sculpture but all the same it's pleasing. I'll feel a swine if we don't win in Krakow, eh, Ed. I agree it's not such a great artistic production but it's an incentive. And it's normal life-size. Why so silent?"

"Yes. Life-size," repeated Lacis. "No, Sergei. It's not there as an incentive. This is a gravestone memorial. It's a sign."

"Your view on everything is too negative," said Gorbunov getting angry, "and I don't much like your wimpishness these days. If the sculpture doesn't appeal to you, don't look at it. Breathe the fresh air, enjoy the acacias. Look how merrily they wave! And the moon's as bright as the sun."

"I can't admire the acacias, Sergei." Lacis never took his eyes off the statue. "You really... excuse me... It's not acceptable of course. But I have one request." Lacis's voice became indistinct. "If anything happens to me, please look after Valentina."

"And what could happen to you?"

"Just now I don't know, but if it should, you will help her, won't you? That's all."

"Now stop it!" Gorbunov felt a lump rising in his throat. "I don't want to hear any more of that. Understand? Happens to him... I should fetch you one across the chops and knock that pessimism out of you. Eh. Shall I?"

"Be my guest!"

"Course I won't. You want it! But I ought to make a man out of the wimp you are becoming. That doctor, you see, throws a scalpel at him and he comes apart at the seams. And when the black parachute opens at 150 metres is he afraid? Words fail me! We'll get home from our holiday, prepare for Krakow and jump. You understand me? So repeat it."

"I've understood you. We're going to jump. Somehow it's all the same to me now."

"Yes, but still," Gorbunov wasn't fully appeased, "This in front of you is not at all a gravestone. It's a statue in front of you, which immortalizes our work. It makes me proud to be a parachutist!" He looked Lacis in the eye. "Proud! Understand!"

"All right. I'm proud," repeated Lacis. "But now it's all over... Look!"

"What are you on about?"

"Look there!"

Coming to meet them along the path was a male figure in a leather jacket.

"You got a light?"

It was Death. Her right hand was gloved. In the bright moonlight there gleamed the rings of a knuckle-duster.

"You should have your own," parried Gorbunov coolly.

"My business is not with you. Move away!" Death transferred her gaze to Lacis and took a step to one side, motioning Gorbunov to go on.

"What's all this then?" Gorbunov inclined his head giving the impression that he hadn't heard.

"Go on. Take off! Get lost." Death again gestured to Gorbunov. "My business is with this hero, not you."

"Go on, Sergei, these are my problems alone. Go on, old man!"

Gorbunov stood stunned for a second or two. Then with a quick blow to the jaw, knocked the stranger into the bushes. Death jumped up, was about to attack Gorbunov but stopped, thought for a moment and then ran off up the path and disappeared. Scarcely a minute passed and the friends had hardly begun to discuss the incident when suddenly a whistle blew and they heard the energetic tread of police feet.

Death again ran up to the parachutists, this time not carrying the knuckle-duster but wearing the red armband of the civil vigilantes and with four policemen following behind.

"Ah so you've already signed up with the vigilantes, have you?" and without further ado Gorbunov knocked the stranger into the roadside for the second time.

Further resistance by the friends was complicated by the numerical superiority of the forces of law and order. Even though Gorbunov did not give in for a long time, and broke away like a wild cat, several times throwing off the policemen sitting on him, inevitably he ended up handcuffed behind his back. And Lacis who had only entered the struggle in a half-hearted way had been lying face down under two sergeants, trying to turn his head and explain that his friend was not what they thought.

All the time Death was running around shouting things, and giving advice to the policemen and whenever possible literally putting the boot in sneakily, now to Gorbunov, now to Lacis. Within fifteen minutes both parachutists were sitting in the paddy wagon and within half an hour staring through the iron bars of a cell in the remand prison.

They could clearly see how the one in the leather jerkin with the armband, and waving vigilante authorisation, was explaining something to the lieutenant drawing up the charge sheet.

For the night the friends were split up into single cells and in the morning Lacis was visited by Death.

"Don't be surprised," Death guffawed. "I just told the guard that we're related. And please be reasonable, today's the day to come to terms about everything."

"You bastard!" whispered Edvardas. "Why is Gorbunov here?"

"Gorbunov?" Death became thoughtful. "Yes, well... Never mind Gorbunov, he'll be all right. He's of no use to me right now. He's not responsible beyond that fight. But you! Well here you are."

Death unfolded a napkin.

"Well now, I've brought some pies for you."

"Take them away. I'm not eating." Edvardas sat on the floor in the corner of the cell looking at the wall in front of him.

"You're making a mistake. They're hot and fresh.

I've just bought them at the stall outside. Eat up. They're not poisoned. Don't be afraid. They feed you such awful rubbish in here. I know it only too well, believe me."

Edvardas took a pie but didn't start on it, kneading it's crackly crust and as before staring at the wall.

"You see, Ed," Death perched nearby and took another pie, "you should understand, consider just how much time out of a good life I have spent on you. All that chasing around. I combed the whole of the Crimea before I found you. Anybody else in my position might have washed his hands of the whole thing. Thought, let him live. Sod him! For me, of course, to think that way is out of the question. Death is death, brother. Sooner or later it gets you... All right, you get one let-off, then another and soon, terrible to contemplate, they'll be laughing at me. It's a matter of professional pride, you know. You think I've got something against you? Nah! I'm really impressed with your love of life. People like you are very hard to get. You know the ones I dislike most of all? The suicides. You want to do the opposite of what they want. It's a matter of principle. Some twit slits his wrists and lies there moaning. He thinks he's passing away. So you hang about over him, and finally call the ambulance! Or the ones who throw themselves under a train. What's it called? Unrequited love. My God. Once because of one of them, I remember, two suburban trains had to be cancelled. But the lovers of life. I respect them. It's more interesting with them. It's even an honour to come to their funerals. To hear the beautiful epitaphs: 'He loved life so much', 'He put up a struggle...' And so on. That's it... Yes... If you're worried about Valentina don't give another thought. She's about to get a promotion at work. And she's going to win a fair whack in the lottery... But that's on condition... You know what."

"You're taking me now?" whispered Edvardas in a doomed voice, "Or will I be allowed to go down to the toilet first?"

"To the toilet... How you all lie, Lacis. I am quite open and he gives me 'the toilet'! He's looking for any avenue of escape. This is a remand prison, not some hotel room with a balcony. 'To the toilet!' I'm not going to do anything just now. Besides, it's risky. They can get you at the exit. We'll finish this conversation and you'll go to your toilet. I have a suggestion. I hear that a parachutists' tournament is planned in Krakow..."

"That's right."

"Well then, get into training. Go to Krakow. We'll do everything there. I'm even ready to take your word for it. As far as Krakow. That's a denouement that suits me. So symbolic. Free-fall parachuting. Sky. The place of our first meeting. Right? Agreed?"

Lacis fell silent.

"And what a nice memorial I've prepared for you. Not the usual little pyramid but like this!" Death half rose to depict a parachutist on the point of landing.

Edvardas shivered:

"The one in that park you mean?"

"Yes. Surely you approve?"

"I do not."

"Well, all right. No great matter at stake there. We can discuss it later. So how about Krakow?"

Lacis was silent.

"You're silent?" Death stood up, took a few steps around the cell and again perched near Lacis. "Silent?... Well then... don't you want to think about Gorbunov?"

Lacis jumped up.

"Sit down!"

"He's got nothing to do with this."

"What do you mean he's got nothing to do with this? What about this?" Death pointed to the white make-up over her bruised cheek. "You could get two years for this. Unless I drop the charges. In fact, it could be much more than two years. If I wanted to, I could get you both hung for murder. You get me? Don't you know that in criminal investigation we have the means to stitch you up easily? A couple of guns planted in the right place. An anonymous informer! Old grandma-witness. That's it. Curtains!"

"Where'll you find your witness?"

"Where will I find one? Ha-ha-ha!" Death was falling about with laughter. "Find one? Why, on any street corner. You know how many old grannies want to live! Ha-ha-ha. So it's a bargain then! You have a choice.

An honourable and beautiful death after a free-fall jump in a major international competition, or a shameful death as a murderer after a humiliating trial and investigation." Death paused. "Together with your partner-in-crime."

"I agree," Edvardas kept staring in front of him.

"Good man. That's the fellow." Death looked at Lacis with respect, and firmly squeezed his limp, now sweat-drenched palm.

Next morning Gorbunov and Lacis were already sitting in their hotel room shut off from the world, celebrating their release.

"What a pain! It almost ruined the holiday," guffawed Gorbunov. Both had had a fair bit to drink. "I thought that's it, they'll lock us up for sure. You know there is surely a kind of destiny, you hear me? Fate has set us, you and me, on the road to Krakow. And we'll go. And we'll win. Surely we'll win, Ed! You remember what I was telling you about that sculpture in the park? What an incentive! And who was right? You or me?"

"You were," Edvardas assented gloomily.

"I should've had a bet with you. Well, Ed, it's destiny. We'll have a clear victory in Krakow. Clear, you understand? Fill them up. Drink up! To victory! I reckon I sorted out that vigilante. We could have still been in the slammer. What I don't understand is what you have been up to, doing any sort of business with that creep. Knuckle-duster, oh dear, how frightening! Ha-ha-ha! But what's his connection with you?"

"I don't know, he must have got me mixed up with somebody else." Edvardas finished his umpteenth glass of muscatel. "I don't know. I know only one thing, Sergei. I know I'm off now to the bath. I'm going to fill it up to the brim and lie in it..."

"Good lad. That's the ticket..."

"I'm going to lie in it, with my body horizontal with just my nose sticking up, and blow bubbles, because I don't want to talk any longer. I don't even want to think, Sergei. But I know this: our national team expects a bigger victory in Krakow than we've ever had before. What's more I know how we'll be rewarded. The award ceremony will be at night. In the moonlight among the rustling acacias. The organizers will bring in a huge ferro-concrete pedestal to fit the whole of our team, with me in plaster at the front, for an incentive... My arms will be raised victoriously. Knees bent. From the harness the iron rods representing the taut rigging lines will be sticking up."

"And the runners-up, Ed, will be the Poles I think," burbled Gorbunov, dropping his head into his plate. "That's because they're the hosts. And towards the hosts as everybody knows... the judges... But frankly, you know. I wouldn't give the Poles even the third place, not on my life..."

Gorbunov snored.

Lacis struggled to his feet and holding on to the wall took himself to the bathroom. With some difficulty he managed to switch on the light and with even more difficulty he took off his clothes. Little by little he established the proper balance between hot and cold water, then slid into the bath. He dropped off immediately, lulled by the even hum from the taps and the gentle lap of the rising water.

He was dreaming of Krakow. The International Tournament. Flags. Fans. Landing strip. The sound of the megaphone. The hale and hearty stride of the instructor. Then suddenly a change in the programme. Instead of the hard landing, a splashdown is announced. And as if from outside Lacis sees his plane having gained altitude and speed make a sharp turn away from the drop--zone towards the artificial reservoir. Lacis is somehow alone in the plane dressed only in underpants, or rather enormous shorts, black with red stripes, but no parachute.

"You ready, Lacis?" yells the instructor over the intercom. "I can't hear you. Are you ready?"

"Ready!" Lacis makes the customary reply, focussing on the water below. Through the engine's roar he hears the splash of water.

"Now, Ed, let's show those Poles!" commands the instructor.

And Edvardas with his usual assured movement leaps elegantly from the aircraft. Everything goes as normal. Several brilliantly executed pirouettes. The obligatory elements are completed followed by freestyle

4*

exercises perfectly executed. There is just the splashdown to negotiate.

Edvardas stretches himself as if to attention as he approaches the water. In the head wind his black underpants inflate like a canopy. His speed slackens. And pointing his toes he slides soundlessly into the water.

With immersion in the water, the roar of applause from the crowd is muffled. The soles of his feet touch the ceramic bottom. Time to come to the surface. Lacis forcibly pushes himself off, but then his head bangs hard against something. Above his head is some kind of wall. What about on the right? A wall! The left? Oh Lord, again a wall! Lacis threshes about under the water losing all orientation. Where's the top? Where's the bottom? He's trapped. Meanwhile his lungs are on their last gasp. There they go, my last bubbles. Well that's it. Goodbye, lads! Remember me kindly. I did my best to win.

Suddenly somebody's hands are grappling with him and dragging him firmly out of the pool. They're slapping him on the back to make him cough.

"Lord. What's going on?" Lacis woke up sitting in the overfull bath. "That you, Valya?"

"How could I be Valya? You practically drowned, you drunken sot. I could tell straightaway."

Death helped Lacis to climb out of the bath and hobble to the ottoman.

"Go on, sleep it off. Otherwise you'll be no good in Krakow and won't even get to the end of your holiday.

Got plastered like an idiot and sank into the water. Who was it gave me his word about Krakow then? Eh!" Death waved her arms dismissively, realizing she would get nothing from someone so mortally drunk, and went off to let the water out of the bath.

"Sure," Edvardas nodded, lit a cigarette and flopped down on the pillow. Dropping off to sleep he was vaguely aware of someone cursing as they took the cigarette out of his mouth and stubbed it out in the nearest ashtray.

During the last days of his holiday Lacis behaved scandalously even in Gorbunov's opinion, to whom Lacis had always been an example.

He drank a lot. Swam far out in rough weather. He would leap from a motorboat at speed. He once started a punch-up in a disco.

He even got into the local nature reserve, paying no attention to the watchman who shouted at him for a long time and finally shouldered his double-barrelled rifle threatening to shoot him. A coarse voice from the shadows had cut him off: "Just you dare!" While the watchman was bickering with someone in the bushes Lacis had coolly picked a bunch of some rare flowers and made off.

He never went on any sightseeing tours, but in the evenings would go down to that park and stand pensively in front of that same statue. One evening he was so drunk that he fell asleep at its feet. But the police found him and took him back to the hotel without charging him.

"What's eating you, Lacis?" Death in a flimsy evening dress approached him one evening in the park. The conversation took place near the statue.

"Nothing. I'm just looking at this statue, this horror. To cheer myself up." Edvardas gloomily examined Death from head to toe, noting the new hair-do and fashionable shoes.

"Been dancing, eh?"

"Yes, and why not?" Death shivered skittishly and seemed slightly drunk.

"Well, successful, were we?" Lacis smirking, continued to examine this thin, angular figure not completely without proportion. "So where's the suitor who's seeing you home? You bumped him off? There must have been one."

"You seem to have a one-sided view of me," Death bridled. "Why must I necessarily be bumping off everybody? Cultural events are not for that. Is it forbidden for me to have time off?"

Lacis again smirked.

"Of course, you can rest after your labours. How was your cultural event?"

"Nothing special. There's this Caucasian fellow pestering me. 'I love pallid girls like you,' he says. He boasts that he has more money than he knows what to do with. He's invited me to his place. What do you think,

Lacis, should I go or not?" With a sly smile Death looked at Lacis, trying to gauge his reaction.

"Oh. Do me a favour. What are you asking me for?"

"Who else can I turn to for advice if not you? We've been acquainted for a long time... but at the same time," Death sighed, "I think we know so little about each other."

Edvardas did not react to this, but turned back to the statue.

"Tell me this," Death's voice took on a severe tone, "why have you been going off your head recently?"

"What have you in mind?"

"It seems to me you're intentionally getting your backside into all sorts of funny adventures. What are you after?"

"Nothing."

"And which devil was it this morning who was crawling over a high-voltage cable. Didn't you read the notice: 800 volts?"

"Yes, but there was no current there."

"That's because I disconnected the knife-switch, you blockhead! What demon's been getting into you?"

"I was going after my cap. That's where the wind blew it."

"God help us. How could chasing a cap justify that? Getting through the wire netting, stepping on the cable... You know, I'm getting worried about you."

"Really?"

"Well, yes."

"Why should you? Why switch off the current?"

"Oh yes, and then who will be jumping in Krakow? Do you want to die like a parachutist or like some dim-witted bystander? You're specially seeking Death? OK, here I am, standing in front of you. Whatever you're seeking, tell me! What are you after? There's nobody about. Speak up! Don't be shy!"

"All right, all right... What can I say, we've agreed about everything... But why are you ticking me off?" Edvardas suddenly went on the offensive. "Are you my mum or something? My wife? Who are you? Ah yes, I forget, pardon me..."

"Lacis, why this tone of voice. Me tick you off? If not me, then who? You've turned away from your wife. And don't look at me like that! By the way, I pity her somehow in a human way. Whatever she's like, she still wants to make it up with you... But you are not interested."

It was indeed true that his relationship with Valentina had soured as never before. To every one of her questions he had one of three responses: 'Yes', 'No' or 'I don't know', and he had not once permitted himself a smile.

One evening Valentina couldn't hold back and burst into sobs, something that had not happened for many years. That day she had bought a pink dress exactly like the one she had worn in her youth, at the time of their first acquaintance.

"How do you like my dress?" she asked, smiling tensely.

Lacis answered: 'Yes'.

"Surely it must remind you of something?"

Lacis answered: 'No'.

"Now think, please, about how we first met."

Lacis answered: 'I don't know'.

"I know it all!" Valentina broke into sobs, soaking her cushion. "I no longer interest you. You men always look for other women at seaside resorts."

"What women?"

"Oh so you think I'm blind, do you? You think I don't see anything?"

"What do you see?"

"The things you've had on your mind all the time lately!"

"I've had nothing on my mind lately."

"You have! Who did you steal those flowers for from the Nature Reserve, eh? I thought they were for me but you went out with them and only returned in the morning... Who did you steal the flowers for? Come clean!"

"For myself. Who else?"

"You mean there wasn't anybody?"

"Nobody!"

"So-o-o..." Valentina half-rose, and, outraged, crossed her arms over her breast. "All right then. Then another question, if you take me for a fool. What about that wench yesterday?"

"What wench?"

"Don't play the fool! You know perfectly well who I'm talking about... Think... Yesterday... Tall, thin as a rake... you got drunk again and fell asleep on the beach and she put an umbrella over you."

"Well, that must have been to stop me getting sunburnt."

"Ye-e-s. There, what a considerate creature she turns out to be. And why you in particular? If that's how it is, won't you introduce me to her, Lacis?"

Edvardas thought for a moment, got the point and snapped, "No!" After that he and his wife hardly spoke at all.

With Death also, towards the end of the vacation there was hardly any conversation. They met only once. By chance. On the beach. Death was standing next to the lifeguard's tent rubbing cream over her sunburnt shoulders and chattering inconsequentially to the slightly drunken lifeguard. He offered a sullen greeting and, scowling, passed on.

Their next encounter took place a month later, in Krakow, after the tournament preliminaries. On the eve of the finals.

"Hello!"

Death stood before him, dressed in a Polish national costume, which Lacis thought revolting, offering him a huge bouquet of flowers. He didn't recognize her at first since she'd been heavily made-up as had been all the participants in the concert programme, usually accompanying sports competitions.

"This is for you, for those wonderful somersaults in the heats," smiled Death. "Really, you jump even better now than when we first met. How liberated you have become. In a different class altogether!"

"And there I was thinking you weren't coming any more," frowned Lacis.

"You sound as if you're not pleased to see me." Death bridled.

"Not particularly. Why should I be?" Lacis took the bouquet and slowly wandered off, away from the drop-zone, his mind full of the next day's jump.

"What gorgeous weather we are having, eh Lacis!"

Death stretched happily, took an enormous deep breath, and looked up at the sun.

"Tomorrow, they say, it's going to be even warmer... But the day after, it's supposed to cool off and be cloudy with some rain."

"Why are you telling me about the forecast for the day after tomorrow?"

"All the same to you, is it?"

"A matter of indifference to me... As I understand it, tomorrow is the day of my last and fatal jump, and you're going on about the weather the day after."

"There you go again! Relax! Your mates are expecting great things from you. World records! And you want to go on about Death. When you jump, you should never think about Death. Think about the mechanics of it. Otherwise you'll lose to the Poles, God forbid!"

"Is it not all the same to you?"

"Of course it's not! I'm on your side. I have to say that I'm a fan of each one of you, not just you. All of you jump very well. So get weaving! I see they've got Jacek Prushinsky on their team."

"Yes... he's good..."

"But you hold the trump card. You're doomed and he isn't. A doomed man must, as never before, experience inspiration. Full freedom of action. He can display the most unbelievable improvisations. 'Aerial insolence' you might call it. Being doomed, as you well understand, means you are not going to hear any criticism from your instructor. Your free-fall time is longer than Prushinsky's, unless, of course, his parachute also jams. Well, are you with me?"

"Yes."

"Now I've got an idea. I think there's no point in you being alone today. I think we should plan a farewell dinner. Here in Krakow they've got this nice picturesque restaurant. Right opposite the cathedral. They serve lobster there. You like lobster?"

"Yes, I do."

"Me too. They take them straight out of the tank and cook them before your very eyes."

"Expensive I dare say?"

"Don't let that bother you. Today I'm paying. I earned a lot of dosh dancing in the crowd scenes." Death giggled.

"Very well, I myself can pay. Let's go."

There can be nothing tastier for a last supper, than a huge Pacific lobster. There it lies with its fantastic claws, reflecting the soft lights from the chandeliers of this luxurious Krakow restaurant. How much flavour and nutrition this magnificent lobster secretes within its flesh! Not only tasty but as beautiful as it is huge. Only an ignoramus would tuck in to it without taking a good look at it first. The inspection is over. The compliments are dying away.

There's the crackle of breaking claws and from them you suck out that amazing juice. But that's only the prelude. There is still the flesh to come. And there is the second claw. A lobster's got two claws. Not one, but two. So there's a sensation of a joy doubled. You eat the first, conscious that there's another to come. And then for the finale you've got the neck. But you're not thinking about that for the moment. Especially since you still haven't finished the first claw. It's enormous. They are so enormous those lobster claws that for any beer drinker half a claw would be quite enough to garnish a beer feast, accompanying the half claw with a mass of cold mist bottles.

The second claw has come and gone. Good! Even sweeter and more substantial than the first. That philosophical question about the meaning of life? Forget it! A real man must plant a tree, father a son, and eat a lobster. How dismayed they look from their portraits those Schopenhauers, Hegels and Kants. You should try lobster, my dear philosophers! No woman could replace a correctly prepared lobster. That's why those envious women bite their lips when they see their husbands dreamily wandering along the sea-front.

The most difficult interim procedure is to break through the armour around the neck. Not just anyone can do it but those who can are well rewarded. However we will put aside the neck question for the moment because it's a mistake to pass to the neck having forgotten the shell over the breast. I've met people who throw it away. Throw them out of the dining room irrespective of their status or rank. To the extent that a man takes pains in dealing with the breast part of a lobster he can be trusted with the most valuable part, the neck. And only he who has passed this delight with honour and at the same time responsibly experimented with the breast shell has the full right to graduate to the mysteries of the fourth stage. He clears away the black intestinal string, moves away the thoroughly scoured breast shell... You ready then? Off we go! Only don't choke! The first lobster can sometimes be the last.

"Well. That's it. I feel I could die now." Lacis happily finished the neck and flopped back in his seat.

"Not die, but perish! Those are two different

things. You should understand that." Death corrected him, with a mouth full of food, and promptly choked. Lacis had to thump her delicate back several times before she coughed up the blockage.

"Ye-es. It's very unwise to eat lobster alone. Dangerous stuff." Death concluded. "Thank you, Edvardas. What would I do without you?"

More wine was brought. Both drank up. Then a prolonged silence. Death lit a long cigarette. Some improvised jazz played and couples shuffled together on the postage-stamp-size dance floor.

"What an evening. We haven't had such a marvellous evening together for a long time. But why so silent, Lacis?"

"What's there to talk about?"

"What do you mean, what? You're a gentleman. Who should do the entertaining, you or me? Go on, entertain me!"

"What, me entertain you?!" Lacis rolled his eyes and roared with laughter. So loud that the headwaiter had to reprimand him. "You?! Don't you have enough amusement? Jesus, you have your fun every day. Someone gets fried. Someone drowns. A third drinks acetone instead of vodka. A fourth... I, for example, have to be smashed to bits."

"You shouldn't talk like that." Death frowned. "I beg you, don't talk about it now... You know, sometimes I hate myself... But there's nothing I can do about it... I do some bad things... But you must forgive me... You must be bigger. You're a man after all. And I'm a woman!"

"What, you a woman?!" Lacis almost fell off his chair laughing so loud that the headwaiter came over again. "You a woman! Ha-ha-ha!"

"And what then am I, in your opinion?" Death bridled.

"God knows what the hell you are. I do know that you are Death. Just Death. You're probably neuter. Or rather... What gender... what sex... Jesus!"

Death looked around the room. Her lips trembled at this outburst.

"There is no neuter gender, Lacis. Understood? No such thing. Indeed, sometimes I have to look like a man and act like one. I have to be cruel at times because life is so cruel. Now pay attention. Nobody ever complains about Death. Everybody complains about Life! And nobody in this life will help you if you don't help yourself. Nobody. You never hear a tender word, let alone have any help... But with you I want to be a woman... Now invite me to dance, Edvardas."

'No, not on any account!"

Death dabbed at the tears welling up. Then stood up.

"Then I'll invite you."

Lacis didn't move.

"No."

"Ladies and Gentlemen," Death shouted out so that

everybody in the dining room could hear. "I announce the next dance will be 'Ladies' Invitation'. Lacis, I am inviting you. Come on!"

Lacis remained still.

"Come on, this is my wish."

With all her strength, Death tugged at Lacis's hand and pressed him against her body. They slowly moved towards the dance floor.

"Tomorrow you'll be smashed up..." Death laid her head on Lacis' shoulder, and lowered her voice to a heated whisper. "I'll miss you, Edvardas. You hear?"

Lacis remained silent, trying to distance himself, but his movements were awkward.

"Kiss me, darling," Death whispered. "Kiss me for the first and last time."

"No! No!" He shoved Death away and with a wide gait, made for the exit.

In the dining room everybody gasped and froze.

"You bastard! You creep! Tomorrow you'll croak. You'll be flattened to a pancake!" screamed Death, chasing after the parachutist. "And generally your team's going to lose to the Poles, and in the individuals, you and Gorbunov and the rest of you will lose to Prushinsky."

"We'll see about that," replied Edvardas, and left the restaurant.

"And do you know what kind of memorial I'm putting up? I'll steal that statue from the Crimea."

Edvardas could no longer hear. He went off to his friends with a confident stride, even though a bit the worse for wear. Thank you, lobster!

The sports plane "Czessna 24" with its full complement of parachutists, having reached the necessary altitude steered towards the well manicured drop zone. Nine of the best parachutists in the land, which included Sergei Gorbunov and Edvardas Lacis were ready to re-affirm their status as European champions which they had won in the last tournament.

The Polish team headed by Jacek Prushinsky had just jumped and gotten good results. Now they were scanning the sky anxiously and enviously at the favourite contenders for the Championship Banner.

"Ready, lads?" called the instructor trying to make himself heard over the roar of the piston engine.

All nine parachutists affirmed their readiness.

"Ready!" "Ready!" "Ready!"

"You look like you're going into battle," laughed Gorbunov leaning into his friend's ear.

Nothing remained of the previous Lacis, relaxed and with an absent gaze. His eyes blazed, his body was tensed like a tiger preparing to attack.

"It's a feeling I welcome!"

Speaking was very difficult, and Gorbunov resorted to a thumbs-up.

"Goodbye, Sergei." Lacis deliberately kept his voice

low so that he could not be heard over the engine's roar. But he felt it to be his duty to say it. He also stuck his thumb up.

"Agreed, Edvardas!" Gorbunov gave the impression that he had heard everything, "I like today's optimism. It's you that's infected me with it, and not me you." He thumped his friend on the back. "That's more like us! Let's keep it up!"

"Weather's good!" Edvardas shouted happily.

"Yes. Good!"

"I gather they expect rain tomorrow."

"What does it matter about tomorrow, you bloody optimist," yelled Gorbunov. "Today we jump. It's the final and he's thinking about tomorrow's weather. Last night the whole lot of us had pre-final butterflies in our stomachs, and they say you were off to a restaurant with some bit of skirt... All right, all right! Sorry. I won't squeal on you, never fear. Just in admiration, Ed. But how did you get on?"

"What do you mean?"

"Well, anything happen?"

"It will today!"

"Maybe she's got a friend?"

They both broke out into laughter in their different ways.

Then the voice of the team coach broke in,

"Well, Edvardas," Gorbunov nudged Lacis towards the exit. "Right, you show these Poles. Off we go!"

One after the other the sportsmen left the aircraft and in no time were all lined up and moving into their team routines, at first forming a circle, then on to other symmetrical figures. One figure, another, a third. Brilliant! Better than the Poles. Prushinsky was biting his lip, watching them through his binoculars... His team mates gloomily applauded as they dragged their gear to the team bus.

The ensemble program had now been exhausted, and to the applause of the fans the group of nine falls apart, at first maintaining symmetry, but then each making for their individual target square in the drop-zone. Now begins the last stage of free fall, the individual numbers.

Prushinsky still has hope, there's still while... But... Jacek Prushinsky gasps and takes his cap off as does everybody else who is observing the display.

Panic in the drop-zone: one of the parachutists has detached himself from his backpack...

Jacek still stares at the sky and understands it all... he pushes off, tortured by the question whether it is worth continuing a career, when your rival is not only more talented, but has no wish to live.

"What are you up to now, playing the fool?" Death in that fluttering shapeless gown, keeping level with the doomed parachutist. "You know I don't like this sort of thing..."

"What sort of thing?" smiled Edvardas, who, now

unencumbered, was performing all sorts of really extraordinary pirouettes.

"A suicide," said Death, clearly agitated.

"And what gives you the idea that I'm going to kill myself," Lacis pushed Death away, who was trying to get closer to him, at the same time cautiously glancing at the earth. "Before the drop I plan to fly up again." And he laughed so loud that it seemed he could be heard in the fields below.

"You idiot," Death frowned, "he plans... On the point of death you joke! Your parachute by the way was normal. I checked it myself. But you unfastened it..."

"That's why I unfastened it, because it was normal. So what is it you want of me? If you're looking for a last dying wish then try this... Put lots of stakes on my landing spot, just to make sure."

"No!"

Death, like somebody hypnotized looked at the approaching green fields and the enlarging mapped-out drop-zone.

"You must fulfil my wish, you creep! I'm counting to three. One, two, two and a half..."

"Your Valya, by the way, is after a divorce!" Death sailed a bit lower, trying to catch the reaction on Lacis' face.

Lacis just laughed and turned his back.

"Look at you. You won't look Death in the face!"

"I don't want to!"

"Coward!"

"Who. Me?"

"Coward! That's a coward. The one who won't look Death in the face!"

"What a little shit you are. Aren't I going to get my wish then? Will you put the stakes then?"

"No! A coward doesn't die so simply!"

"Right. I'm counting to three... One, two, two and a half, three!"

Lacis darted forward and seized Death's floppy gown.

"Who do you think you're calling a coward?"

He raised his hand to give her a good hiding... but lingered for a fraction of a second too long, as if undecided... Something restrained him, held him back... His raised right arm fell limply. Then he found himself in the grip of a tenacious embrace. And two cold clammy lips fastened on to his.

"Let me go!" he muttered, "Please let me go!"

"No. Now I get my wish. You had yours last time."

Lacis was immediately tossed upwards: the usual state the parachutist experiences when the canopy opens, and somewhere down below came the sound of an ambulance siren and despairing cries.

The parachute had opened at a dangerously low altitude and Edvardas' feet painfully hit the earth of the well-trampled centre of the clearly-outlined landing target, even though he had bent his knees in good time. But that tight embrace did not relax...

For a long time, pulled by the wind, they were dragged by the black parachute across the grass...

The New Romantic

The huge bomber was flying in the night sky above the sleeping city. The pilot in a black helmet gazed heavily at the controls of this military aircraft. It was carrying a bomb in its hold. A huge black thing shaped like a massive teardrop. Complete with a stabilizing mechanism to assure accurate aim. Below, the city lay spread out with its square and semicircular humps of concrete apartment blocks.

"If I release this lever," the pilot was thinking. "If I let this thing go... Then my bomb... My huge black bomb... Will crash into the thick of this concrete city and scatter every living human thing lying below these wings. And if I don't? If I don't release the lever... Then my plane will just go on ahead with its steady four-engine rumble. And will hurtle into the countryside mists."

In one of the houses in that same city a scientist

was unable to sleep. Not sleeping but listening to the approaching aircraft's rumble.

"Yes, that's it!" he thought, "Just imagine," thought the man of science. "In the night sky... In the night sky of this city a machine is flying!" And he dashed on to the balcony, straining into the starry sky his piercing inquisitive gaze.

At some moment their eyes met. The heavy sullen gaze of the pilot. And the inquisitive gaze of the scientist, full of unexpected thoughts. The pilot's hand was held back. It didn't release the death-dealing lever.

"Brother!!!" shouted the pilot into the space of the bomber. "My own brother! Dimka!"

"Evgeny!" The scientist also recognized his brother and mentally greeted him.

The night-bomber hovered over the balcony with muffled engines. The scientist waved to his brother, and settled down at his desk to complete his monograph.

In a certain courtroom. In a certain gloomy courtroom. In the columned hall of the court martial... The sentence was being read out. The final. The harsh, The irreversible. The jurors were sitting behind a table with a decanter. The depositions of the witnesses lay on the green cloth.

"For treason against the motherland," the judge proceeded. "For betrayal of your country. For negligence in fulfilling your air-force duties," the judge's voice rose. He collected his thoughts so as to be able to pronounce

the condign punishment. But something stopped him...
It wouldn't let him pronounce the death penalty.

"Father!!!" A painfully familiar voice rang out from the dock.

"My son! Is it you? Alive!" the reply resounded.

The handcuffs fell off. The escorts cheered, rejoicing in this unexpected re-union. They had much to remember sitting at the green-covered table with the decanter, now on this occasion full of some strong stuff. This, in the court martial room.

But there was a certain sergeant Fakhruddin two floors below who did not join in the singing and celebrations two floors above. He was pacing up and down between cells from which prisoners' arms reached out. He, Fakhruddin, didn't want to hear their multiple groans, curses and prayers.

Thirty-five there were. Thirty-five relatives of Fakhruddin languished on his right and left in these cells. Thirty-five of his starving relatives, stretching out their hands, begging for bread and water. But Fakhruddin just paced up and down, up and down, rattling his keys. The only time he stopped was when he reached the end, where he had to turn around.

"Shame on you, Fakhruddin," sighed the writer who was hiding at the end of the corridor. "What are you doing, Fakhruddin? What does your callousness create? You've got your wife in Cell 17? Yes, Fakhruddin! In Number 9 you've got three sons! Have you forgotten that or something? How many times have I told you about your brothers! Shamil... Niaz... Seranji... Can you hear me, Fakhruddin? You pace up and down and don't hear? Has your head been turned by the captain's promise of a medal? Why don't you grab the keys and free them all, or tear at the cell bars blistering your hands. Do you hear me, Fakhruddin?"

The writer hung his head low, and fell to pondering. He had no right to go further. Pen and paper, alas, are the new romantic's only weapons.

The Sniper

After he was demobilized, the sniper Shokotov, having walked some 200 metres from the garrison gates, climbed a pine tree and camouflaged himself.

The lookouts on the garrison tower, astonished at the sniper's rapid disappearance, scrutinized with their multi-magnifier binoculars the whole length of the road that led into the civilian landscape. As did the sniper from his tree-top position, with his pale blue eyes and pinpoint pupils.

Three days later the garrison security men found Shokotov, hauled him out of the tree and drove him to the train station to send him off to his native village. They revved up the car engine, produced their tobacco stash and clowned merrily. Only the escorted Shokotov kept silent, peering into the evening lights of the station through narrowed pale blue eyes.

They settled Shokotov into a reserved seat. The colonel personally sent a telegram firmly ordering that the sniper be met, then he ordered his team back to the garrison as time was getting short. The car set off for the garrison as the train raced away to the village, full of passengers glancing through the windows at the landscape flashing past. Even more attentively scrutinizing the latter from his top bunk, was the retired sniper with his pale blue eyes and pin-point pupils.

All the Shokotov family and other villagers who had assembled on the platform were shouting joyful greetings, "Shokotov! Sniper Shokotov!" At this moment the train attendant was shaking the sniper, who was lying under his blanket, glaring at the attendant with his pale blue eyes and pin-point pupils, persuading him to get out.

At home Shokotov was greeted as a hero. A feast was prepared in his honour: a roasted wild boar, chicken and all sorts of other delicacies. "Modern Talking" played cheerfully as the Farm Chairman recounted the farm's achievements to the becalmed, preoccupied, retired sniper.

In the night the demobilized sniper disappeared. He wasn't to be found in the cellar, the attic, anywhere. Three days of bewilderment. On the fourth day behind a stone at the roadside. the stableman Polikarpov stumbled on the camouflaged sniper Shokotov.

From the stableman's account to the village assembly, "He's lying behind a stone. Quiet and staring. Those eyes of his, pale blue, and the tiny pin-point pupils. Optics!"

Hardly anybody in the village slept that night. And anyone who did, dreamt of one thing: pale blue eyes, four rifle cleaning rods and a skillfully riddled target.

After three days the agronomist Sharafetdinov lost his double-barreled rifle. At exactly the same time as the loss, the retired sniper Shokotov disappeared. Shortly after this the village ploughman Tolstikov noticed that a large beam, sticking up at the edge of his field, had begun towards noon to lean more to the left! He jumped off the plough, dropped his whip, abandoned his horse to the devil and shrieking "Shokotov!" fled into his hut and stayed there.

Salt, soap and matches disappeared from the local store. Vegetables were grown in trenches. People wasted no time in their shopping. Smokers didn't hang about in the streets. The pop of a car exhaust would have the physically fit dropping instantly into a road ditch, frozen to the spot, gazing blankly at the sky. The enormous pale blue sky. With its endless pale blue eyes. With its pin-point pupils.

Security Guard Song

To Security Guard Parakhnyuk his duties meant more than mere "security". He would crunch out the word fiercely, "Secc-yurr-ity!" with respect, with power. As if preceded by a drum-roll and the command "Hah-tairn-Shun" showing off its epaulettes,

> With measured pace
> The legendary Special Task Force,
> A glittering amalgam
> Of fierce eyes
> And iron bodies,
> Marches off to secure
> A most important objective.
> And the General, the greying hero,
> Presents an engraved watch:
> "Wear it, Parakhnyuk."

How could this ever make any sense to those scientists and engineers who staffed the research institute policed by Security Guard Parakhnyuk?! They couldn't even pronounce the word 'security" clearly. No rasped 'R's, but to Parakhnyuk's fury a slipshod, prissy "Skoorty".

Shooting was too good for them!

"Your Pass!" Parakhnyuk would demand. He pronounced it harshly, cruelly: "Passss!" It was more than a mere pass to him both in form and content. Like a glittering pennant on his breast pocket. With a drum-roll in the background,

> With measured pace
> Marches
> The legendary Special Task Force,
> A glittering amalgam
> Of fierce eyes
> And iron bodies.
> And the General, the greying hero
> Presents an engraved pistol:
> "Good man Parakhnyuk!"

How could this make any sense to the scientists and engineers who couldn't even do something as straightforward as producing their pass? They would fumble in their pockets for a long time and then show it upside down. There were several who regularly left it behind and muttering "The bastard!" would wander off home.

Shooting was too good for them!

Once Security Guard Parakhnyuk had a dream accompanied by drum-rolls.

> With measured pace,
> The firing squad leads
> To the show execution
> A young scientist with sloppy speech

He could not pronounce clearly the word "Security", and instead of his pass, produced his travel card. "Allow me," said Parakhnyuk to a drum-roll background.

> Without a single miss
> He lodged eight bullets
> In the head of the oaf, the criminal.

"Eight-Zero" applauded the General presenting him with an engraved machine-gun.

The next morning was for Parakhnyuk the first when everything seemed to fall in its proper place:

> His wife had dressed in military fashion,
> The baby's cries were clear and precise.
> The trees had been trimmed tidily
> Along the pavement
> Where Security Guard Parakhnyuk,

Strode with measured pace,
To occupy his post.

Half an hour on, and late for work, the Junior Research Fellow slouched in, the very one from Parakhnyuk's dream,

"Oh yeah! Skoorty," drawled the jerk lazily probing his pocket for papers. He dug around for a long time and found his travel card and various receipts, took them out. Looked in the other pocket... Finally he pulled out the crumpled pass, and started in surprise: "What am I doing with my wife's pass? Come on, Skoorty. Let me in. It's all shit anyway?"

In Security Guard Parakhnyuk's head, the drums began to beat: "Still alive, the bastard..."

And the flock of doves lifting off from the Guard House, flew across to the tiled roof of the neighbouring building. Which to be honest was scarcely visible through the morning mist... Still visible, yes. If you look with a clear gaze!!!

The Divan

Having slopped around that boggy countryside for several days, Ivanov, Sychev and Kalugin came upon a divan. It was brand-new, soft, and looked a very pleasant resting place. And of course completely bizarre in the middle of this endless boggy wilderness. But the travelers were too exhausted by their sleepless journey through the unending mud to give any thought as to why this divan should be there. It was there and thank God! All three perched on it. Groaned. Immediately all three had this urge to sleep. And here was the problem. The divan was small and, naturally, could only accommodate one sleeper. No room for the others even to sqeeze in on either side. So a plan was drawn up; one of them would sleep while the others would either stand nearby, or walk around in the vicinity. Our heroes cast lots and Kalugin was the lucky one. He stretched, then threw himself on to the divan, bounced on the brand-new springs a little and promptly fell asleep.

"Two hours. Then we wake you." Ivanov squeezed the words through his teeth, and set off on a stroll somewhere close by. Sychev preferred to hold his ground and stared enviously at the sleeper, and as Kalugin continued to sleep like a log, began to express his envy out loud:

"Sleep you bastard, sleep... Ten minutes gone. One hour fifty minutes to go. So." He had his eye fixed on the second hand all the time, "An hour and forty seven minutes left."

When there was an hour and a half to go, Ivanov returned.

"How long now?"

"One hour twenty nine minutes," Sychev calmly replied, not for a moment taking his eyes off the second hand.

"What do you mean?" Ivanov turned green, "I feel I've been walking around for a whole hour, if not one and a half. Gor!"

He looked at Sychev's watch and waving his hands turned round and wandered off again. He returned once more, his eyes swollen with fatigue just fifteen minutes before Kalugin was due to be roused. Sychev was also getting no fun, standing stiff as a statue at the head of the sofa. He ground his teeth, glancing now at his watch, then at the sleeper.

"Well then, what?" He showed his watch and breathed heavily. "Let's toss for the next sleep."

Ivanov, who could just about keep himself erect, simply could not conceive the possibility of losing, and then either wandering about or standing like a statue for another two hours. He looked at Sychev as if at somebody who had actually had his sleep out.

"If I lose I'll simply collapse into this sludge and choke, because I couldn't walk another step."

"Have you thought about me?" Sychev was in a sweat in spite of the cold.

"I've been standing here for two hours, like an idiot staring at my watch. I'm already seeing double."

"All right then don't stand. Take a walk," yelled Ivanov, swaying. To him it already seemed that the dice had long been cast and he had won, but that Sychev had dug his feet in and wanted to cheat.

"But you know, don't you!" Sychev suddenly had the idea that when Ivanov had wandered off he must have found a similar bed not far off, had a quick sleep, and come running back for another spell. "So where've you been?"

"Over there in the bushes."

"Right then get back there and sleep as much as you like. And by the way, there aren't any bushes growing in this bogland."

"Oh yes, so you'll know what sort of mud you get there, won't you? Look at my feet. Look at that mud."

"Shut up, will you, lads, I can't sleep. It's been so peaceful without you," babbled Kalugin in his sleep.

'Get up, you bastard. Time's up!" Sychev glanced at his watch and although there were still four minutes to go he began to pull Kalugin off the divan.

"Get up!" screamed Ivanov joining in, crashing on to the divan like a felled tree and with what strength he had left, tried to push Kalugin off the divan.

"Get off. Go on, get off." Kalugin grabbed the felt upholstery so tightly that his fingers went blue, and he kicked out at the invaders.

All three of them were so preoccupied with each other that they didn't notice the approach of a stranger behind them.

"Hi! My name's Tarasov." He roared like thunder from a clear sky.

"This divan belongs to me. Look, I've got the documents to prove it."

The man smiled and opened a folder with some papers. All three leapt up and without saying a word threw themselves at Tarasov trying to throttle him into the mud and scatter the cursed documents. But it wasn't easy to get the better of Tarasov. He was healthy, ruddy and it was evident that he had slept well. He extricated himself, got to his feet, gathered the documents and threw off the clinging hands of Ivanov, Sychev and Kalugin, then slumped on to the divan, thrusting the document folder under his shirt.

"What a bunch!" Tarasov said with a shaming glare. "Blood was spilt for the sake of that divan, and you wanted to appropriate it."

"What do you mean, blood?" The three of them stopped in their tracks, ready to listen.

"Well, it's like this!" Tarasov turned on to his back, put a hand behind his head and unhurriedly began his tale.

"This is how it was... We were withdrawing from Burashev, as the Germans approached and their artillery pounded at us almost point-blank. We had lots of wounded, and the commander ordered me and another sergeant to find some sort of bed or ottoman for our injured political officer.

Ivanov, Sychev, and Kalugin, holding their breath listened to Tarasov's long, highly dramatic tale, snorting heavily from time to time from the piercing wind, or shuffling from foot to foot to avoid being sucked deep into the mud.

"Well after about a year we liberated the village and an order was made assigning the divan to me." Tarasov completed his story and again showed them the documents. "And you lot wanted to take it over."

Ivanov, Sychev and Kalugin turned away without saying a word and squelched through the boggy slush with drooping heads, not looking each other in the eye.

"Listen," Ivanov broke in after an hour, "It's been a half century since the war, and that divan looks brand new."

"There are some things that never age." Sychev explained philosophically. "My uncle has a plush armchair, a war trophy. They say it's a hundred years old and it still looks as if nobody ever sat in it."

"An armchair... a wonderful object!" Ivanov agreed dreamily, "you can just sit in it, or stretch out in it and sleep. A hundred times better than an ordinary chair. They're hard to find these days, and one that isn't occupied..."

"Look!" Kalugin broke in, 'Look!" and pointed his finger.

On the horizon against the background of the purple sunset beyond the endless, borderless bogs they could see a lonely camp bed.

The three exhausted travellers set off towards it...

Billy Goat

Literally everybody called Fedoseyev 'Billy Goat' — his neighbours and workmates and even his wife and children. Once his two-year-old son Alyosha who had barely started to speak yet looked out from his cot and, putting his hands to his head like horns, squeaked: "Billy Goat!" This was too much. Fedoseyev marched into the kitchen shouting: "Varya. What have you been teaching this kid?" and gave her a clout. Varya burst into tears and swore that it wasn't her. She loved her husband and did not want to upset him.

"I couldn't have possibly called you that in front of the kids? Calm down. Don't be so bad-tempered, you silly-billy. You're just tired after work."

That night he asked her,

"Listen. I just don't understand why they all call me Billy Goat. You, for example."

"God knows," she whispered, stroking his hair, "Remember when we first met I nicknamed you that right away."

"You must have heard it from someone."

"No I didn't, I swear. The first time I saw you, truly."

"So why did you marry me?"

"I fell in love and married you. That's all."

"OK, but it's still puzzling somehow. My mates at work, for instance. What makes them call me that? Don't they respect me at all?"

"Stop making things up. You know they respect you. It's just a nickname. Let's get some sleep now!" And they dropped off in the middle of a kiss.

Everything should have been all right. They had a nice home and good earnings. The children were obedient — they did call him Billy Goat, but they still obeyed him. Generally speaking life was normal. But the nickname gave him no peace. "Why Billy Goat?" Every day he looked at himself in the mirror. His face was broad, handsome, clean-shaven. Nothing goaty about it.

"Hey, you silly-billy," his wife would say, putting her arms around him, "you keep looking for a likeness? Relax and don't think about it." She made the bed.

Fedoseyev decided to take his holiday in the country so as to have a look at real goats and work out the resemblance. Straight away he approached the chairman of the collective farm.

"Where is it your goats are pasturing?"

"What's it to you? Who are you anyway?" answered the puzzled chairman, then peered closer at Fedoseyev screwing up his eyes. "Oh yes, I see. Yes! Up there on the hill." He looked as if he wanted to add something but then held back. "Up there. Go on there."

So Fedoseyev climbed the hill.

"Look, lads," chortled the shepherd, seeing Fedoseyev. "We've got a new recruit."

"Who are you talking about?" asked the worried Fedoseyev climbing up the hill.

"Glad to see you, mate!" said the shepherd not bothering to answer and casting a professional eye, looking him over from head to toe. "Fancy meeting you. Where did you blow in from?"

"I'm on holiday. From the town. Came to look at the goats," he blurted out, staring at the shepherd and preparing for an extended conversation.

But the shepherd only smiled and nodded for Fedosyev to follow him deeper into the herd where within a minute the newcomer was whirling and frolicking among the goats, as if weightless and unaware of his legs, talking about town life and the latest political events.

Alpatovka

Somewhere up in the Urals there is a village called Alpatovka. Nothing special about it. It's just an ordinary village with about two hundred houses. Although it's been there five hundred years it's never managed to grow into a town. Next to it is a deep, dark forest — a scary kind of place... But really, it's just like any other forest you typically find in the northern Urals. However, throughout those five hundred years of Alpatovka's existence, people have been disappearing into that forest.

Back in the age of Peter the Great, rumour has it, Prince Menshikov himself once rode into the forest and lost half of his men there. The Czar had him badly beaten for that. As for the rest of Russian history, everyone will of course remember from their school textbooks what Bashkir chieftain Salavat Yulaev said to the peasant king

Emelyan Pugachev: "O Emelyan! I have brought you five thousand Bashkirs!" That's what he said, isn't it? Well, you see, the truth is there had been in fact ten thousand Bashkirs, not five, but half of the troops happened to have marched through Alpatovka... And so the story continues, right up to the present day.

During the Civil War, old timers recall, a whole Red Army battalion hid themselves in that forest while fighting the Whites... and never came out again. True, years later, after the Second World War, two weird old characters wearing Red Army caps and ragged jerkins once emerged from the trees; stood for a while on the edge of the forest, smoked a few pipes, and then went back in. But who the hell knows, maybe those two guys had nothing at all to do with the lost battalion. Maybe they were just two old men who happened to be wearing those caps and jerkins.

In Alpatovka itself there isn't now one complete family, that is, not a single family in which at least one person hasn't disappeared somewhere along the line. Families in Alpatovka tend to be large — ten, fifteen members or more — but as a rule, after a few years five or six of them have gone missing. People in Alpatovka are fairly relaxed about this. The forest kind of regulates the size of the village's population. The same goes for cows, chickens, geese and other animals. Of course, there is theft. One can't say there isn't. But although on the one hand things do seem to get stolen, on the other it's not as if they really are. It simply isn't proper in Alpatovka to notice theft.

Say, for example, a man had stolen a goose from another man; well, even if the other had actually seen the goose being stolen, he would never say a word, and he would go over to the first man's house to dine with him on that very goose. People in Alpatovka don't like to make accusations. The victim of the theft would come to the thief's house and they would eat the goose together.

"Eeh," the victim would sigh, "One of my geese's gone off today."

"What?!" the thief would reply in amazement, ripping off large mouthfuls of flesh from the goose leg. "Went to the forest, I s'pose?"

"S'pose so."

"Well, well..."

And so they would go on eating the goose together, both knowing perfectly well which goose this was and where it came from. But in Alpatovka, to make up any kind of explanation apart from the 'forest' alibi is simply bad form.

"You know what, Fyodorov's goat went to the forest the other day. And that was the end of it."

"You mean nobody found it?" the owner of the goose would ask.

"'Course not! What are you talking about? I'm telling you it went to the forest."

"Oh, well..."

And so they would go on chatting, even though just the day before they had together stolen Fyodorov's goat; even though the victim, Fyodorov himself, had witnessed the theft through a crack in the door of his outhouse. But that same evening, as if nothing had happened, Fyodorov would go along to dine on the goat with the two others and complain about that 'devil of a forest.'

True, in the case of people the forest was indeed partly involved in their occasional disappearance. From time to time somebody's wife would get murdered, or a troublesome son strangled. The body would be taken to the forest, and that was that. The murderer would hurry to the local police officer to report the missing relative.

The police officer in Alpatovka was just the right sort of man for the job. He could read and write, and he was conscientious. He would carefully document every piece of evidence. Then he would walk up to the forest, stay there for a long time, take some measurements with a measuring tape; then he would fill in a report, open a new file, and keep the file in his safe.

"So? What happened to my wife? Where is she?" the murderer would ask a year or two later.

"We'll find her, we'll find her, don't worry!" the police officer would answer encouragingly, and he would continue filling in forms and putting files in his safe.

As for the police officer himself, he had a passion for horses. Nearly half of the horses in the village were in his stables. But his greatest pride was a light-chestnut racer. Six months earlier Semakin, the blacksmith, had had exactly the same racer... but somehow it had disappeared.

"He went off to the forest, and never came back!" the blacksmith had complained to the police officer. "Ran away the bad lad, his mane tossing in the starlight!" Although the blacksmith had seen very well from behind his own barn how things had been in reality. It wasn't at night that the horse had disappeared, but early in the morning. And there had been no stars the day before because of the clouds. "You should have been more careful with a horse like that, Mike. Should've treated him better!" the police officer would say to Semakin; and he would take him down to the stables to show him the light-chestnut racer and give a lesson on how to treat him well, stroking the horse's mane and feeding him wheat from his hand.

One day the police officer had a bit of bad luck himself. The safe containing all his files and documents disappeared, just the day before a certain Commission of Inspectors was supposed to come from the city to inspect Alpatovka.

"This is no tragedy, of course," the police officer was saying, trying to reassure himself and the village men whom he had called up for interrogation. "But you know, a metal safe running off to the forest all by itself — that's not really possible!"

"Well, officer, you never know," the village men ventured. "On the one hand, true, it's a metal safe, like — it can't move, but on the other hand, y'know, all kinds of things can happen..."

"Yeah, like my old woman, she lay around in bed paralyzed for two years, and then suddenly last spring, off she went — just disappeared, without trace!"

"Oh yeah, I remember that story, I remember," said the officer scratching the top of his head. "Took me three days to investigate it. That devil of a forest swallowed her up, that's what it did! Just swallowed her up!"

"That's it, that's it, swallowed her up!" the village men cried, rejoicing at the appropriate turn of phrase. "So, y'see, maybe that safe of yours... maybe the forest... sort of... swallowed it up? Eh? What do y'think?"

"Maybe, maybe." The police officer kept pacing up and down from one corner of the room to another. "But still, that city Commission, are they gonna believe that? I sure hope nothing bad happens to all of us because of that Commission."

"Aw now, come on, officer, why worry about a commission? They'll never get through to us anyway, and if they do, they'll never get out. The forest is deep and dark. You know that, don't you?"

"Whether they believe it or not, don't worry, officer! All kinda things've disappeared in our forest — whole squadrons, convoys... And you're talking about a commission? You gotta be kidding!"

After the men left, the police officer sat down at his desk and wrote a letter to the regional police headquarters questioning the need for the Commission of Inspectors to come at all. Glancing out of the window from time to time, he watched, smiling, as the neighbour's little boy shook down all the apples from his apple tree.

Eventually the Commission did get to Alpatovka, with no particular problems apart from the loss of a suitcase containing canned food, which somehow sank itself down into the swamp one night. Upon their arrival the starving inspectors went straight to the village shop, deeply astonishing the lonely and bored shopkeeper. The shopkeeper was even more astonished by the ten-ruble note that the Chairman of the Commission extended to him, asking him to bring up "the tenner's worth of food". The shopkeeper silently took the money, went away and never reappeared until closing time. Actually 'closing time' didn't mean much in this case since the door didn't fit the frame, and there was no lock.

The inspectors decided not to waste any more time and, full of shame, picked some plums from the trees along the way. The owner of the plum trees saw all this perfectly well. Cutting through backyards he ran ahead of the newcomers, then came walking towards them and asked them if they would spare him a few plums. He inquired where they were going and offered to accompany them. As he walked on with them, and while the Chief

Inspector shamefully looked down at his feet, he told them of how he himself had been trying to grow plums just like these, but that they had been disappearing lately because of some strange sort of 'forest creatures' that would come out of the woods at night and steal away all his harvest.

"Welcome, dear guests! Welcome!" cried the police officer greeting the visitors astride a light-chestnut racer and dressed in parade uniform. After one failed attempt he managed to stop next to them, jumped off the horse like a sportsman, and introduced himself.

"Now let me invite you all to follow me down the main street."

The inspectors obeyed and walked down the village street, admiring the police officer's uniform and wondering at the great number of medals he wore.

"We have this tradition you see," the police officer went on. "Whenever we have guests in Alpatovka, we always start off by taking them down the main street."

"Why is that?" asked the Chief Inspector, surprised.

"Openness. The traditional Alpatovka openness. To avoid suspicion or mistrust. Let everybody know who has arrived, how many people, what for, and, well, all the rest of it, and then, if (God forbid, of course!) anything should happen to you, then everyone, even the tiniest little kid, will be there to help you. Eh? How's that?"

The inspectors smiled and nodded.

"When there are no secrets, people are also more

hospitable," the police officer continued, patting his horse's mane. "There are fewer crimes, and it makes life better. Isn't that true, Semakin?" he cried out to a rather sad-looking man with a beard who was standing behind his garden gate and observing the procession. "Out here in the sticks, people are revealed for what they really are, just like in battle. The man who never says a word, who stays all closed up inside, is a lost man."

"Do many people get 'lost' in this way?" a member of the delegation asked, jokingly.

"Quite a few," said the police officer, and he tightened his reins to restrain the horse." I remember I wrote you a letter about the forest, didn't I? Get a chance to read it before ye left? Well, then so you'll know. But of course, you've only got our word for it. It could be just us who think somebody's disappeared. We see that from our own local point of view. But in reality, God only knows. Maybe it's the opposite, maybe that guy's found himself somehow. Maybe right now he's sitting out there in the forest, in a hut, cracking nuts, untroubled and quite content. Master of his own fate."

"Of course, of course, anything can happen... Well, well..." said the Chief Inspector thoughtfully. "But, if you'll excuse me, officer, wouldn't a person like that give some kind of warning to the other villagers before leaving?"

"Usually, they do. If they have time, that is. `The forest is calling me, I'm going', they say. And before you know it, they're gone. By the way, you yourselves, on your way here, didn't you get that kind of feeling? You didn't? Strange. They say it draws people, like a magnet."

"No, no, quite honestly. We didn't."

"Well, thank God for that. Because I'd promised to all Alpatovka that your Commission would come. You know, I'd made all those promises, and then I started thinking to myself: but what if they don't make it, what if they don't make it? But in the end you did. Hey look, here're some more of our people."

It was the shopkeeper and a certain Fyodorov, a stocky man with distinguished grey hair. They had been running to catch up with the procession and were both puffing and panting. Interrupting each other, they told the police officer how they had just been trying to catch a pig that was escaping to the forest from Potapov's shed. Potapov was well known in the village as the best pig breeder.

"It must've been bored sitting there in its shed all the time. Potapov wouldn't let it out for days on end. So it tore off two boards from the shed and ran away to the forest."

The police officer gasped and shook his head.

"Dear, oh dear, what can we do, what can we do? Thank God it's only a pig that's disappeared, and not Potapov himself. Where would we find another pig breeder like him?"

"By the way," said the shopkeeper, lowering his

eyes and kicking the ground with the end of his foot. "Would you care to try some Alpatovka roast pork? See, it just so happens that Fyodorov and me have decided to cook some dinner... Kinda coincidence... You shouldn't miss it."

"That's true, you know, the odd plum's not going to fill you up." Fyodorov supported him, looking the Chief Inspector straight in the eye.

The visitors glanced at each other and looked at the police officer. For a minute the police officer wondered aloud whether to go and hunt for the pig immediately or to take care of his guests. He chose the second option, and told a loutish little boy who came running past, hiding a red rooster underneath his shirt, to go and look for the pig.

The guests had just arrived at the shopkeeper's house and sat down for dinner, when Potapov appeared at the door, white as a sheet.

"Hullo, folks, do you know, looks like one of my pigs's gone off to the forest. Broke down two planks in the shed and ran away."

"Terrible" said the police officer, frowning and spreading a napkin over his chest. "But, why don't you just sit down and have some dinner! Your pig can't go too far, don't worry. You can give me a full description?"

"Sure."

"Fine, then! Just sit down and tuck in."

And the police officer wrote down something on

his notepad. Potapov gave a deep sigh and began to eat some pork, glancing every now and then at Fyodorov, at the shopkeeper, and at the little ivory elephants which decorated the sideboard at the other end of the room.

The Chief Inspector took a stern look at all those sitting around the table and said, breaking the silence:

"I should expect it'll be a rather difficult job to find a pig if it has really run away to the forest."

"Very difficult, of course. Who said it would be easy?" smirked the police officer. "It's the forest, you know, not just a house. Full of bushes, hollows, thickets... And that's only part of the problem. Just think — what if the pig suddenly got stuck up a tree?"

"What do you mean, up a tree?" said the youngest inspector, almost choking on his food. "What sort of pig would climb up a tree?!"

"I didn't say it would climb up a tree," said the police officer, putting away his notepad. "I said it might just get stuck up there. Remember your suitcase with the food — you didn't drown it in the swamp yourselves, did you? It just sank down by itself, right? Well, there you are... Now if a suitcase, being a thing without a living soul, suddenly sinks into the swamp by itself, why shouldn't a living pig suddenly find itself on top of a tree? Y'know, there it would go, quietly trotting along, and suddenly it would just get taken up there. And then you go try and find it in a place like that! You'd be lucky if it even made a sound... but what if it suddenly fell silent? It might keep quiet, poor thing, maybe at the very moment when we'd be all out searching for it."

"Yeah, it's true," Fyodorov joined in, wiping his mouth with his hankie. "Anything can happen in that forest of ours. It's as if — you know — as if it were alive!" He gazed in awe out the window at the pine trees in the distance. "Hear that noise it's making?" See how it's waving its branches? I'd swear to God it's alive, I would! And the things it gets up to... Things that not every human being would be able to do. It's under-standable, in a way. It gets bored, you see, the poor green thing. Us people, we live our lives, we work, we grow things, we do well. But the forest, if you think about it properly, also wants to have things, poor devil. All kinds of things. Our job is to guess when he's due. To know in good time, when and what that old forest's gonna swallow up. To understand it, and then lay it on, off your own bat. Yeah, that's how it should be!"

"That's right. Once I had a white grand piano," said the gardener, the owner of the plum trees, suddenly joining in after a long silence. "Bloody beautiful! And how it played, how it played! You'd hear it right across the whole village! And suddenly one day I felt like the inspiration'd gone. I played on the white keys, and somehow the music wasn't right. I tried the black keys, and they weren't right either! And then, the neighbours started to complain. They said to me, take it to the forest?

Take it out there by yourself. The forest likes music. It'll always take your piano, no problem. I looked out the window and I understood. The trees were rustling and waving their branches. They were claiming the piano. I felt really sad, but what could I do? So one day, off we went with the whole family and took the piano way, way out into the forest. And do you know what? It accepted it! The forest accepted my gift! Since then I've been to that place time and time again, and never once did I find the piano there. But you know what? You can still hear the music coming in, every now and then. Listen, hear it now?!"

Indeed, the sound of piano music came floating in quite clearly to the ears of the guests.

"By the way, d'you remember, how many suitcases you lost on your way here?" the gardener suddenly asked the visitors with great animation. "Only one? That's not much. That's really very little, you know, for our forest! I tell you, if I were you I'd go out and leave a couple more there, just for politeness' sake, like. It's up to you, of course, but if you ever come round to the idea, please let me know, will you? I can show you a place out there. No devil in the world'll ever find it. And then, some time, in a week or so, you might well get your reward."

"What exactly do you mean by that?" the inspectors asked, and they stopped eating and began to count their suitcases.

"I mean just that. You know, you lose a suitcase,

but then, say, you might find a bride in Alpatovka. You wouldn't say that's a bad deal, would you?"

"Yeah, that's it. Why not?" said the police officer, supporting the gardener, and he winked at the youngest inspector. "The forest, you know, it doesn't just take things. It also dishes them out. Understand? This forest's very generous."

"Look at these trousers and jacket I'm wearing? I got them from the forest," added the shopkeeper for no apparent reason. To prove it, he stood up and showed off his fancy suit glistening with spangles. "Here's how it all happened. First, the forest swallowed up my wallet, my ceiling lamp and the odd bit of crockery. I worried and worried. I kept looking out of the window at that mass of thieving greenery. Then one day a messenger came to the door. Go to the forest', he said. `Just go straight there, don't turn around. No point in hanging about here. So I went. I wandered about, looking at the bushes around me. You find all sorts of rubbish lying around there: an empty wallet, a watch without a dial... And the forest kept getting denser and denser. It was as if it was luring me in. I thought I'd go a little deeper. So I went on. And suddenly, a pair of pants hanging on a tree! I went a little further, and then — a jacket! I put them on and ran back as quick as I could, before the forest could change its mind. And now, see, I'm dressed up all nice and smart! No one else in the whole village has a suit like that!"

"Knock it off will you! Stop showing off," said Potapov the pig breeder, interrupting him and looking sadly at his soiled frock-coat. "Or else you might have to give it back. And then everything would fall back into place, you know."

"No, no! Things are quite alright as they are now. Aren't they?" said the shopkeeper looking at the police officer.

"Maybe, maybe," said the police officer, still listening to the piano music." Pity though, you didn't go a little deeper in. I really have the feeling that if you'd gone right to the middle of it, you'd 've found a tail-coat," he said with a smile. "But well, never mind, never mind. As for the piano, I'd be hardly surprised if in a couple of days someone else in the village received a piano just like that one. That's of course, if they haven't got it already."

"Me, me, I wouldn't mind it!" cried the shopkeeper. "My wife's been taking music lessons."

"What do you mean, your wife? You haven't got one. She went off to the forest three years ago, didn't she?" said Potapov, remembering.

"Yeah, well, she could come back, couldn't she? Maybe she's playing the piano just now. Keeping up her skills, y'know. She might've been walking in the forest, and then suddenly she saw a piano, sat down, and now she's playing. Maybe she'll come back when the piano is back in this house. She'll come back, she will, when that beautiful piano is standing here again! Right here, in that corner!" The salesman pointed to an empty corner in the room.

"Well, well." The Chief Inspector coughed, stood up to have a look at his suitcase, refused a glass of vodka, which was being offered to him and sat down again. "And what about the authorities? You know, the authorities, the District officials... Do they come often this way, to have a look around?"

"They do, they do quite often," said the police officer, sadly looking at the murmuring trees. "But they don't all make it through to here. You see, people get scattered about the forest. They can't seem to manage to concentrate on one pursuit. Some like mushrooms, some like to go berry-picking. Some even get stuck up in pine trees. Once in a while, one or two manage to get through. But what use are they if they haven't got any suitcases? They're no good to anyone — except, maybe the women! So they decide to settle down here and make themselves at home, and maybe they're right. You can't get the hang of a place in one quick visit, can you?"

"I say, do you think I might be able to meet any of those people? I mean, of those who did manage to get through?" the Chief Inspector insisted.

" 'Course you can. You won't need to go too far, either. See Fyodorov here in front of you? He's an army general."

"General Fyodorov," Fyodorov introduced himself and held out his hand to the Chief Inspector.

"Shevchuk," said the Chief Inspector, looking at the General in amazement. "May I ask what branch of the service? If it's not a secret, of course."

"Tank Corps." Fyodorov answered firmly. "We don't have secrets from each other here in Alpatovka."

"What do you mean tanks?" said Potapov, deeply surprised. "What d'ye mean, tanks when there's a rocket lying in your vegetable garden?"

"So what?" said Fyodorov, buttoning up his collar and scratching his grey hair. Maybe the forest swapped me a tank against a rocket. What business is it of yours, anyway? Before there was a tank, now there's a rocket, that's all. And besides, where the hell would I find enough fuel for a tank?"

"But somehow you found enough fuel for the rocket, didn't you?"

" 'Course we did," said the salesman, supporting Fyodorov. "I've got as much rocket fuel in my shop as anybody could want. It's just that no-one here buys it except General Fyodorov. You see."

"It would be better if you had a few groceries in that shop!" the Chief Inspector could not help exclaiming as he remembered his visit to the shop in the morning. "Your shop has a sign saying `Groceries', you know."

"What d'ye think it should've said: `Strategic Ammunition', or what? When the door doesn't shut and I can't get a lock? No, no, I'll leave it as it is — 'Groceries' — it'll be much safer that way, I'm sure."

They went on eating and drinking for most of the day. Then they sang songs about dear old Alpatovka. Fyodorov and the salesman, interrupting each other, told different versions about the origin of the village's population. The gardener kept counting the suitcases. The police officer drew the visitors a map of the shortest route through the forest, in case they wanted to go back. And Potapov went walking back and forth across the room, rubbing his hands and, little by little, so that no one would notice, pushing the sideboard towards the exit.

Suddenly, when it had grown dark, a loud neigh was heard from the street. It seemed to come from the light-chestnut racer that had been tied to the gate near the house. The police officer listened. But through the window everybody could already see Semakin galloping past the pine trees, leaning down on his favourite horse's neck and kicking him in the sides with all his might.

"Well, time for me to be off," said the police officer, and he looked sadly at the guests, collected their passports in order to fill in the registration forms for their visit, and went out. The inspectors were given a room for the night, with a window giving on the pine forest. By then the large Alpatovka moon was already shining on the tops of the pine trees.

"There's something I don't like about having left our suitcases in the living room," said the Chief Inspector. He had some trouble falling asleep, and kept smoking and walking around the room. "And those passports — we ought to have handed them in tomorrow morning instead. I can't imagine they're going to do our registration forms at night, are they?"

"Oh well, what difference does it make, whether it's at night or during the day?" said the youngest inspector, looking out the window indifferently.

"Well, it certainly doesn't make any difference now," the others agreed, and they all began to fall asleep.

"Let's sleep on it. The night will bring counsel."

"Actually, uh... My dear friends," said the Chief Inspector, still not able to settle down, and he lit another cigarette. "I've been wondering all this time whether I should tell you... The fact is... Of course this is not going to sound very professional of me, but... Well, in short... Again, I shouldn't want you to understand me wrongly..." And with trembling hands, he pulled out of his pocket some small objects, which made a dull clinking sound.

"Here, you see..."

Everyone saw the little ivory elephants that had been standing on the sideboard during the dinner.

"When I came out of the living room, I... well, in short, I just nicked them off the sideboard. No one noticed. But this is just for a deposit, my friends, just a deposit. And of course, it was hard to resist the temptation. Such a beautiful collection. But again, I beg you to understand me correctly. If anything should happen to our suitcases, at least I'd have this collection to — er, you know... as a compensation, sort of thing. Please understand me correctly. That's it."

"Oh, come on, Inspector, don't apologize." The Deputy Chief, whom everyone thought had been sleeping, pulled out from under his pillow the police officer's leather briefcase, held it up for all the others to see, put it back under the pillow again and began to snore.

"It's true that the night brings counsel," said the younger inspector, still looking out the window. "Good Heavens — a white grand-piano! Now I think I understand, at last. I can see now where that music was coming from. That's where it came from! From the east side."

"What d'you mean, white? It's light-chestnut..." said someone in his sleep. But it was already long past midnight, and nobody felt like arguing anymore.

The Jiginka Bream

A fishy tale from the Kuban

If you want to catch a bream from the Jiginka River don't forget to bring a lash. A good strong lash that cuts the air with a whistle when a sturdy arm swings it way back as the tip crackles and hisses.

There's absolutely no point in going after the Jiginka bream without a lash.

And be sure to bring your horse too. No self-respecting Cossack would ever fish bream with a rod and tackle.

A horse, a lash, and a bottle of good hooch, the kind that makes the sky tilt if you take too big a slug. And the second slug that tilts it back but at another angle. But then after the third slug, it's time to get moving.

Whether they are biting or not, you'll get him if you're a real Cossack!

Like that one over there charging into the river with a dashing air, on his trusty steed Arsenal, whose mighty breast forges a passage through the reeds.

The horse is now up to the saddle in water. On it sits the Cossack. So where are you, bream? No sign! Nothing visible. Not because he's not there. He's hiding. The bream fears the Cossack. He's tasted the lash and the Cossack's prowess many times before, when he got tangled up in a net, as he tried to get a hold on the horse's bit. Not to mention the other fish or the local Muslims (*Busurmans*) who crouch in the reeds coaxing the smaller fry on to their hooks. The water has settled now and the river is quiet. The Cossack is rooted to the saddle, but he isn't asleep. Meanwhile the bream is creeping up stealthily behind and the ripples raised by its huge bulk are approaching the horse's rump. But the Cossack can't see it. A busurman sitting on the bank sees it all and cries out.

Like a scaly moon the fish rears from below the surface, and with the full force of its body muscles deals a mighty blow at the Cossack's back. But the Cossack holds on in the saddle. He permits himself another slug of hooch. His response is to set about with his lash until the water's frothing all around the horse's rump. The lash cuts up the river surface. Another one of the locals on the bank takes fright, cries out, and makes off into the moonlight carrying his fishing line. This heathen will not return here to torment the smaller fish.

Meanwhile the bream has taken refuge on the riverbed licking his wounds, but not giving in. He is wondering whether to have another go at the Cossack or drag off the third busurman by his leg. That's the one who is wading up to the ankles well away from this sinful affray to collect his crayfish pots. But no, the fish is too slow to catch this cowardly local on the shore. No, this one throws his tackle into the water and flies off like a bullet, back to safe territory to wander round the bazaars spinning yarns about his exploits. Yes, it would have been good then if the fish had grabbed the busurman, but he can't make it. So he swims back to the Cossack... Sideways on, straight for the horse's belly to tip over both horse and rider, then tear them apart and gobble up his eternal foe in the water. Then ploughs along the slime of the riverbed like a cruise missile.

The Cossack's wife sighs in her sleep. Darkness falls over Jiginka. A black cloud covers the solitary moon. A wind is starting up, slanting the ripe corn. Sudden gusts bend the unbreaking stalks, the heavy ears touching the ground. It is going to be a good harvest in Jiginka. The Cossack is holding out against the fish.

The horse can feel the water's movement, the heavy lap of the waves from the monstrous back of this devilish bream. And it whinnies as in the good old days when it used to warn its sleeping master of the approach of thieving foreigners, Muslims, Germans and what have you. No matter who it is, a Cossack can deal with anybody as long as he's awake. The Cossack tugs the reins and he and Arsenal shift sideways so the bream flashes past like a torpedo, sending up a big wave. Then his lash hooks on to a fin like a lasso on the mast of a Greek barge. "Hold it! Think you're sneaking through the green channel eh? Hold it!"

There is just a whistle as the fins stand out, big as saucers, and cries and shouts from all sides. Only this time it isn't the Greeks making the hubbub, but the third and fourth Busurmans, beseeching Allah to get them out of this cursed Jiginka. They aren't much interested in either the bream or the Cossack. All sorts of other fish are rising to the surface: perch and burbot, stunned by the noise of the Cossack's lash. They are of no interest to the dashing Cossack but they do interest the fifth Busurman, the one scooping up the water with his cupped hands on the off-chance that he can land some of the stunned small-fry.

Down at the river's end, questions are being asked. "What on earth's going on? Why this turbulence? After all it's not a waterfall, not the Volga. It's our own Jiginka! Why the foam? Why the water's rage? What have we done to offend our great provider?"

That's how they were thinking down at the river's end, those honest fishermen. They thought one thing, then another. Then they took their caps off and thought again. Having done that they had a good drink. Then a pensive snooze. After all it was night. Those Kuban fellows are a thinking bunch. They can leave anything else to other people. But not the thinking. They do their own thinking. That's what those fishermen are like down at the river's end.

That sixth Busurman would have seen a terrifying sight, had he not taken off after number five, drooling at the prospect of the small fish delivered to the shore by the big wave. These natives will squabble over the burbot but that's of no account. Any deals will be done far from the actual events.

But this terrifying sight has been left behind. Only Busurman number seven witnessed it. Not because he was daring. But because, terrified, the poor sod was rooted to the spot. Paralyzed, holding his expensive foreign-made multiplying spinner.

The bream gets a hold on the saddle, rips off the belly-band and drags the Cossack into the depths. A terrible whirlpool swirls in the middle of the river as fish and Cossack disappear from view. The loyal steed whinnies. It has many times come to its master's rescue. Now it dives using hooves to stamp at the bream's fiendish snout. This, just as the Cossack's fists have gone into action, hammering away to right and left at the fish's gills and teeth. The Cossack is now astride the fish. "Forgive me, Arsenal!" Air is running out and his strength is failing. But the bream is not what he was in former times, when he would drag away a calf or even one of the farm pigs, much to the delight of the Jiginka farm chairman who is on the fiddle. The animals would arrive from the towns every year, sometimes from Moscow, sometimes Petersburg. Together with the grain, they were stolen by the herdsmen and the loss put down to the bream's depredations. The Cossack is now putting a stopper on all that.

Realizing now that even under water the Cossack is a bigger threat than any fancy net or hook, the despairing bream tries one final evil strategy. He pretends to surface, belly up, while keeping a sharp look out. He pretends he is being dragged submissively along the shore but he signals with his tail to the other bream in the water.

They gather in a semi-circle. Snarling. Their monstrous eyes are glittering. They are smacking their lips now at the Cossack, then at the horse. They swim towards them but not too close. After all who knows how many other Cossacks may be lurking in the dense Jiginka reeds. And perhaps the ill-digested Busurman meat has made them sleepy. Or maybe there is a lack of that esprit de corps among the bream population that you get with the Kuban Cossacks. Carefully, softly-softly, they inch forward. Meanwhile the Cossack doesn't even bother to turn round to face them. But continues to drive his fish with all his might, taking a final pull from the bottle. He's not going to waste good liquor when clouting this stupid fish over the head with it.

It's already morning. They rise early on the Jiginka. Even the loving couples have gone home from the fields. At this point the cock would have crowed if it hadn't gone into the casserole the day before, instead of the hen.

Now the sun is coming up. The rising sun illuminates the Cossack's lonely pillow. That pillow's seen a few things in its time. It's been tossed about by naughty Cossack children. It has done duty as a pregnant belly for dressmaking. It has been burnt by a hungover sleeper's cigar. It has been brandished against intruding farm animals and used to gag blathermouths. Yes it's seen a lot. Above all, this pillow remembers the Cossack's sorrowful head. Not that the weary Cossack actually needed the pillow's support. His wife would put it under his head without raising the rest of him. And he would snore on that pillow till dawn after cursing his wife. And with the dawn he would fling the cissy object into the corner.

"Off you go, softy!"

And then flop out again.

But at this moment the Cossack's mind's not on any pillow, as he drags the great fish to the river bank, nor is it on the farm chairman who will soon be in jail. Nor on Busurman number eight, who right now is prancing along the road to Jiginka hoping to do a deal. No, the Cossack is wondering if any frying pan exists that could possibly accommodate the Jiginka bream. Or an oven that it could be baked in. Even if you got a sufficiently large imported job it would still be no good. The bream would stretch the thing to the limit and test the toughness of German nuts and bolts. So the Cossack is going to dry it, hanging between two poplars. And when the nosy gangs from the pub ask him about it he'll reply:

"Oh that! Just a tiddler!"

Boomerang

The boomerang is a terrible weapon. A boomerang comes back. If you ever should chance to throw one of these whatsits — take care!!! Do a bunk as quick as you can! Because when it's hit its target it always slews round and with a whistle, scuds towards the exact spot where your head should be. Even if you manage to leap round a corner that's no guarantee of safety. If it doesn't locate you the first time it can do a sharp sideways turn and land you a terrible wallop. But even that's not all. It can thrash and clobber you till you're begging for mercy. You do so in vain. A boomerang knows no pity. Even a boomerang lying on the ground can quite easily jump up and tear into your trousers, or in its thick-witted mania get up speed with its strong wooden blades and cynically slap you about the face.

I often recall an occasion when a group of weary

workers were sitting and singing, waiting till the rain was over. When suddenly from behind thunderclouds a flock of black objects looking at first like a wedge of birds appeared in the sky and hurtled towards them with frightening speed. When the situation dawned on them and they ran off in all directions it was already too late. The boomerangs not only struck people on the street, they caught them in the landings as well. Several of them dislodged glass panes and burst into apartments. One woman trying to save herself from the boomerangs shut herself in a cupboard not noticing that one of them had softly-softly slipped in with her. But when she locked the door it jumped up, and with a wild whistle set about mincing her up together with the clothing. So they buried her with the cupboard, thinking about the living.

But not all boomerangs are a threat to man. Some of them only cut off treetops as they cruise peacefully in the night sky. Some quietly glide over the grass. There are a few who pick away at the earth. Some say that the Japanese have learned to throw them down mine shafts to hew coal and return to the surface. In this sense the boomerang has a future. You've just got to instruct it to use its natural talents, its diabolical twists and dynamics of aerial flight.

I can imagine a peaceful harvester throwing the boomerang under the ripe ears of winter and spring crops. Yes, also a warrior, standing up for creative labour. He

can guard a frontier, with his boomerang lodged in a
special holster. He can guard from his concealed hideout
the whole of the open sky. Ready and coiled at any
moment to strike the aerial target, this camouflaged
boomerang-interceptor.

Laughing Lenny

Lenny would have his fits of laughing in the most inappropriate places. His roaring laughter made the walls tremble, crockery would rattle, and a chandelier might even shatter if they had a chandelier where Lenny was seized with a laughing fit. Finally, he would collapse among the splinters of broken glass and would lie face down until the medics would arrive picking their way through the debris and take the exhausted Lenny to the intensive care unit.

Lenny didn't understand jokes, was unmoved by cartoons, was unafraid of being tickled. He laughed only rarely in fact. But always quite suddenly! And as a rule in such inappropriate places, that people were afraid to invite him anywhere. Never to their birthday parties. He was freed from attending business meetings. Banned from May Day demonstrations. He would try to go with the others, but stopped by the police cordon, he'd move away dropping his flag and the paper flowers he had usually made himself.

Once a well-known satirical writer/performer who was putting together a new show took the risk of inviting Lenny to his first night, in the hope that his laughter would prove infectious and ensure his success with the public. The public made not a sound. Everybody looked at Lenny in horror, as he sat silently in the front row, watching the satirist breaking out in a sweat struggling through his doomed act.

After the ruin of this public idol, Lenny became even more fearful. People stopped telling jokes, laughed more rarely, and generally tended to keep off the streets. Even the police, once they encountered Lenny on his evening stroll, preferred to find somewhere else to patrol. And Lenny with his collar turned up, would wander the town's vacant pavements in total silence, his sorrowful eyes scanning the shuttered windows and grey walls of the buildings.

Time in the city flew quickly. Summers differed little from winters, or days from nights. The flat hills surrounding the city rarely echoed with any sound. And only occasionally terrifying bursts of guffawing, the sound of shattered glass, and the crash of fallen objects reminded of the fact that the town was alive.

Hobbies

Police Sergeant Makhnovecky devoted all his free time to dancing. Even after the Police Dancing Club had ceased to function, Makhnovecky would lock himself in the dance hall and go through all the steps, perfecting his dancing technique. "Slow. Slow. Quick-Quick. Slow. One, two, three. One two, three." Makhnovecky was a joy to behold.

Lieutenant Shevtsov loved singing. He would sing on moonlit nights between police assignments. "La-la-la." His voice wasn't bad.

Now Captain Solovyev was out of luck. He didn't have a hobby, and had nothing to show off about. He skulked and snarled at everybody. He would sometimes try out the "slow-slow, quick-quick, slow" routine, but Makhnovecky would simply sneer at him. He would strike up a song "La-la-la", making Shevtsov wince.

"Why am I so untalented?" grieved Solovyev, chucking his boots away as he arrived home. "I tried fretwork but that was no good. I bought an accordion but that didn't work either!"

His wife was very sympathetic but she hadn't a clue how to help him. She simply sat with him and sympathized as she watched him eat.

Once they had an assignment to get three armed criminals. They had to apprehend all the three by any means.

Makhnovecky overtook one of them, danced around him and kicked him you know where, after which he took him off to the station. The criminal writhed.

Shevtsov to be sure wasted no time either. "La-la-la," he sang, fumbled for the appropriate melody and then pounced on the second criminal.

But poor Captain Solovyev was out of luck. God had given him neither a good figure nor a voice. He chased after the offender calling to mind first his fretwork, then his accordion. Then attempted to sing and to dance. But the offender drew further ahead and the bullets flew wildly off target. So what's the point of having a bloody weapon if you've got nothing else to your name? Disgruntled he threw the gun away in despair, sat down and suddenly wrote a poem.

The right thing to do! Within a week the runaway criminal killed himself.

"Hey, you've made it," laughed Shevtsov and

Makhnovecky encouragingly, "You've found yourself. In fact we thought of getting you an easel or something of the sort."

"An easel? No, not for me, it should be for Major Kurbanov. He draws. But me... no." He became thoughtful and the other two tactfully slipped away.

A new quatrain was being born.

Sablin and Sologub

"**K**eep still, Sologub!" Sablin raised his pistol and aimed at him.

"Go on, shoot, you bastard!" yelled Sologub at his opponent.

"I'm not a bastard," Sablin bridled, "and this is an honest duel. You've already had your shot. Stop moving: I kept still when you were shooting."

Sablin fired and hit Sologub in the arm.

"Oh! Oh!" Sologub writhed, holding the elbow of his wounded arm until the pain eased, then loaded up and took aim at Sablin.

The shot resounded loudly, a great deal louder than the previous one. Sologub was about to rejoice (for the shot had the healthy sound of a winner) when he noticed that Sablin was still standing up in one piece. He almost fell over in dismay.

"Did I hit you?" queried Sologub, feebly hopeful.

"No," replied Sablin. Calmly, as if dealing with some abstract question. "No. That seems to be that." Sablin pushed aside a lock of hair from his brow, so as to have an unimpeded view when firing. Then he fired and Sologub fell down as if polaxed.

"Ah! Oh! Ah!" howled Sologub who had been hit in the hip. The pain was unbearable and he scrabbled across the grass trying to stifle it.

Then, propping himself up on his good leg he took very careful aim at Sablin.

"Sablin! Kiss the world goodbye." Sologub pressed the trigger so brutally that it seemed as if not one, but a dozen bullets would fly from the black barrel.

"Hello! What's going on?" Something in Sablin's clothing had seemed to twitch as the shot resounded. "What's going on?"

"You missed." Sablin stood still as if nothing had happened.

"But what about your jacket? I saw it move!" Sologub was hoping that Sablin was just hanging on and would collapse at any moment, lifeless on the grass.

"What about my jacket? It could have moved in the wind. There was a gust of wind at the moment of firing and you got the illusion from that."

"It moved from the shot!"

Sologub wanted to run and check if there was a wound. But both the pain in his hip and the strict rules of duelling prevented this ("it is forbidden to cross the halfway point until the end of the duel.")

"If you'd hit me I wouldn't be chatting with you now, I'd be writhing on the ground and all the rest of it. So stay still." Sablin very carefully aimed at Sologub and fired. The pain was colossal.

"This terrible pain!" muttered Sologub, "terrible pain."

He lay on his back looking at his last cartridge, which he must fire to finish off Sablin once and for all.

"Dear little bullet," he entreated, "strike Sablin, kill him! Rid this earth of him!" He rolled on to his stomach, and steadied his shaking hand to take careful aim at his target. He fired. The expected result did not materialise. Sablin remained standing.

A moment later Sologub died of loss of blood, wounds, and dismay.

Sablin returned home from the duelling field, his brows knitted as he went over every fiendish detail of the contest. His shooting had been significantly superior to Sologub's so all in all no doubt should remain. But... there remained one small detail... Sablin had not played straight. He had been wearing a bullet-proof vest, and he had definitely felt the blow of a bullet. This occurred with the third shot when (remember?) his jacket had twitched. He examined the jacket carefully. Yes, there was a small hole just about the level of his liver. So the bullet-proof vest had saved his life. "If it hit the liver," he thought, trying to justify himself, "it wouldn't have killed me, I'd still have kept the upper hand."

But all the same he came home in a depressed mood.

"So you won then?" His father shouted from the kitchen.

"Yes, generally speaking..."

"What do you mean 'generally speaking'? You killed him?"

"Yes."

"OK. Good lad! Why so miserable then? You killed him and thank the Lord. Eat your lunch or it will get cold. The important thing is that you won and not him."

Sablin ate his lunch sluggishly, all the time looking at the hole in his jacket, but making no mention of it to his father. After the meal he locked himself in his room and stayed alone there for a long time. A couple of days after his opponent's funeral he decided to visit the grave.

It was a cool day. There was nobody about except Sologub's wife.

"Hello," Sablin smiled guiltily.

"Oh, it's you," the woman turned back to arranging the flowers around the grave, then stepped aside with bent head. "That looks better. What brings you here?"

"I don't really know. Some sort of shame maybe."

"Why shame? You won honestly in an even fight. It was a duel after all. Either you him, or him you, one or the other. So?"

"Can I be of any use to you?" Conscience was nagging Sablin, who kept thinking about the bullet-proof vest hanging in the wardrobe. "Can I offer help, make some amends...

"Well, if you've got the time," pondered the widow, comparing her husband's grave with the others, "OK, the grave fence needs painting. You could do that!"

"Of course, yes, of course," Sablin was happy at this chance to show sympathy.

And already by the next day the paintwork was resplendent with touches of gold. The victor had not stinted on money for quality paint on Sologub's grave.

But after another week even his handiwork proved weak consolation. Often, in moments of drowsiness, he would remember that twitching of his jacket caused by Sologub's bullet, the agitation, and the powerful dull thud that shuddered right through the whole of his metal vest.

"Ach! Sod it! I cheated!"

Then he would come round. In the subsequent weeks he wore a pinched look. He frequently dreamed about that bullet. It would take flight, strike the vest at that same place over the liver, flying off and twitching his jacket. Then, as if having second thoughts it would return, crawl over the bullet-proof surface, seeking a breach or a margin and tickling its way through, then jump under the skin and lodge in his liver. Just in that very place... After this Sablin would wake with a cry and jump out of bed.

It's hard to explain why, but lately Sablin was often involved in duels. Practically every day he was at it. But what's more, before the duel started, he would now ostentatiously strip to the waist and walk in the open towards his opponent, smiling, obviously wishing to demonstrate to himself that he had turned over a new leaf.

"Why do you do that?" one opponent asked him, as he was dying, looking at Sablin's sunburnt torso. "After all it's so cold..."

"Well it's a sort of compensation..." Sablin couldn't explain what he meant by this, couldn't find the words, besides which he had to get his breath back. The duel had just finished and had been a very hard one, and both of them were breathing heavily, Sablin sitting on a tussock and his opponent bleeding to death on the grass.

Nothing could help Sablin to get the duel with Sologub out of his mind. Even in multiple duels with a large number of participants and victims, when in the chaos of flying bullets you might forget your own mother let alone Sologub, Sablin would look a bit confused. Weary and pensive, he would despatch one opponent after another, naked to the waist, his mind flooded with the memory of that twitching jacket and that bullet's thud trembling through the entirety of the bullet-proof vest.

"Come on, put this on!" Sablin once offered his metalled vest to an experienced duellist. Who donned it, surprised. They paced away from the flag. Sablin shot him in the head, killing him outright. This way he lived with his oppressive thoughts. Already several years had passed. But one day, walking through the cemetery past the glittering fence around Sologub's grave, his nerves gave out...

He ran home, donned that very jacket and shot himself through that tiny hole into which that bullet had once lodged itself on its way to the liver. He woke up in hospital with a doctor sitting by his side.

"Where did this happen to you?" asked the interested doctor, preparing a syringe.

"Where, where — in a duel, naturally."

"I see." The doctor injected him and was about to go when he suddenly spun round and, putting his face close to Sablin's whispered heatedly,

"What kind of idiots are you? What goes on in your head when you're shooting, eh? Surely one of you would have had the sense to wear a bullet-proof vest!"

"What kind of bullet-proof vest?" countered Sablin, going pale.

"Look, this sort!" The doctor unbuttoned his gown, then his shirt to display a brand-new bullet-proof vest. "Go on, look! Us doctors also fight duels. You can't avoid it. But we use our heads."

"What if you get the bullet in the head?" Hiding

his aversion to the man with difficulty, Sablin decided on a little further elucidation.

"Ha-ha, brother, we've got another line of defence," He took off his cap and showed a massive metal hemisphere, "Look at that, you twit!"

"And if you get a serious thigh wound?"

"For that possibility we are also armed," The doctor laughed and pulled his trousers down to show his armoured legs.

"Right, you bastard, we'll meet in the morning", Sablin bridled and turning on to his side he slept peacefully. No twitching jackets, or stupid dreams about wandering bullets disturbed his rest that night. Early in the morning a ward orderly took him in a wheelchair to the site of the duel where everything, pennants, pistols and other requisites were in place. The doctor stood there, nervously chewing his lip, naked to the waist, wearing only shorts and with nothing on his head.

"I see you haven't bothered with your gown" mocked Sablin, checking his weapon, blowing through the barrel as custom required.

"That's so you can see I fight fairly," the doctor muttered. "You'd have checked anyway. Why would I want a gown now."

"That's right, you won't need one any more." Sablin also stripped to the waist, adjusted his bandages and began to hobble towards the starting point.

"Get ready!" ordered the second, a young orderly.

Sablin took aim well, and let fly, convinced that the bullet would immediately fell his enemy (he had raised his game considerably as a result of recent shoot-outs). But the bullet flew so slowly that you could simply sidle round its path.

"Go on, faster!" Sablin stamped his foot to which his liver responded with a stab of pain. "What's it doing, going so slow?"

"It's not destined to hit me," laughed the doctor watching the approaching bullet.

It was approaching so feebly it was never going to inflict any damage on him. He was in no hurry. Mockingly awaiting the bullet's arrival, the doctor, ostentatiously proffered his chest and even took a step towards it. But the bullet, turning aside, rid itself of all momentum and dropped to earth.

"But I... But surely I hit him!"

"Here you are! Take this!" The doctor took aim and with a single shot blew Sablin's head off. "That's him for the cold room!" ordered the doctor getting his things together and going off for his gown.

Sablin was dead. He was buried and the grave was covered with flowers. Everything just as it should be. But it was impossible to understand one thing. Why did the bullet travel so slowly? What sort of mysticism was at work here? And why on the other hand did the doctor's bullet blow off Sablin's head? It was only an eight-millimetre. Eh? Perhaps the doctor will be able to help clear the matter up. But at the moment, he is chewing his lip, and making his way into the cemetery to paint the little fence around Sablin's grave. With gilt paint. Having left his patients in the care of his devoted orderly and second.

Love

Somehow the engineer Kharitonov could not manage to get married. The reason was very simple. The women who fancied Kharitonov were unattractive to him, and the ones he fell for didn't fancy him. "What a bugger!" he thought, "Why can't we gel like it happens in novels and films? After all, requited love has got to exist somewhere!"

Catching sight of a woman he fancied, Kharitonov would leap at the opportunity to see her home, as a rule as far as the porch, where he would be given to understand that no further meetings would take place. He was beginning to feel like a nutter. Sometimes he could get a few minutes' relief by shouting insults at the latest temptress. And routinely he would go home glancing gloomily at the passing, usually ugly, wenches making eyes at him.

Again and again Kharitonov turned to novels and films. From these he learnt that to succeed, you had to show persistence and passion, or even perform some heroic feat. "Right then, we'll start at the beginning. With persistence," he decided, and he set off to accompany the latest beauty with whom he was vaguely acquainted. But evidently sick of him by the time they reached the bus stop she declared, "Thank you. I can manage on my own now." Then flew into the bus. "Aren't we going to meet again?" Kharitonov yelled after her loudly but uncertainly.

She smiled and turned away to the ticket machine. Kharitonov hailed a taxi and told the driver to follow the bus. He felt ashamed, but remembering yesterday's film with its happy ending in which the hero's "persistence" played a crucial role, he resolved to press on to the end.

They passed about ten stops without her getting out. The driver, whom Kharitonov had instructed to slow down at every stop, and whose irritation was expressed in a less than delicate manner, kept asking "Now what do you want?" Eventually she got off the bus at the last stop and turned her head at the torrent of filthy language the taxi-driver flung at Kharitonov who had paid him only what was on the meter. Kharitonov, red in the face and unsure whether to retort or not, closed in on her saying: "I told you we'd meet again."

Without a word, she started running away. Kharitonov, with a guilty smile on his face, set off in pursuit, wondering how in his place an experienced film lover might respond. To his great chagrin, he found she was belting along and the distance between them scarcely closed. The race was nothing like the carefree lovers' pursuits Kharitonov had often observed in films. Yelling at her back as reassuringly as he could he combined assurances of his lack of evil intent with the information that he would soon be promoted to a senior engineer, and that generally speaking she should not be walking alone on the streets so late. Having cried out all that he got completely out of breath and fell well behind. So he covered the rest of the distance between them in pensive silence. It was now too late to turn back — they had some mutual acquaintances, she could tell them all and ruin his reputation for many years to come. There was only one way out. He had to catch her up and win her heart, or at least beg her not to tell people that he had been chasing her.

Passing a line of rubbish bins, stinking the way they never do in any novel, he put on a spurt and broke the rhythm of his quarry. Just about twenty metres away from her house entrance she tripped and fell, banging her head on the pavement.

It was a moonlit July night. Twenty metres from the apartment block, a beautiful young woman lay on the pavement, loudly weeping, her forehead bleeding. In the windows of the dark apartment block, the sleepy tenants were looming, offering to call an ambulance.

Around the young woman's slender body Kharitonov was fussing, trying to make a head-bandage out of his handkerchief, oopsing and apologizing each time he accidentally touched her anywhere apart from the forehead.

Itching

At three in the morning Sychikhin's back started to itch. At first very slightly as if he was being bitten by tiny gnats, then more strongly, and finally quite fiercely as if some mice were gnawing away at him. Removing his shirt he rushed to the mirror, crunching his neck round to examine his back. Nothing was visible apart from the reddish marks his fingers had made during the night on the white mounds of his well-developed muscles. Baffled by this ailment he composed himself and went back to bed. But then the itching intensified so much that he dashed back to the mirror, fell over and smashed it. There was no time to sweep up the splinters. His back was itching so much by now, that he knew if he didn't deal with it he would go out of his mind.

Jumping about and almost weeping, the enraged

Sychikhin began to scratch with both hands, and when they got tired and numb, twisted round his back, he fell on to the corrugated rug and writhed, digging his heels in and pressing his elbows into the floor. The rubber rug didn't so much help as give out indecent burps, thus aggravating his suffering. So Sychikhin had to relinquish it, and jumped up again, stretching to his full height. With his last ounce of strength he managed three times to scrape across his back till his knuckles were blue, as if hoping that his physical exhaustion might also bring the end of this stupid plague.

Just then a fly settled on his back and crawled around. Sychikhin dealt it such a mighty blow that he dislocated his right shoulder and now he could only scratch with the left hand. He had no strength to scratch any more, merely going through the motions now. His fingers could not clasp anything, and his swelling right arm hung uselessly. Suddenly with the arrival of pain in this limb, the itching somehow or other died away, and the joyful Sychikhin carefully moved into the bathroom to bathe his right arm in cold water, chanting out loud reassurances: "It's gone! It's gone! It's gone!" Then, catching sight of a poster featuring the rock singer Sting, his wife had put up the previous evening, he fell silent, broke into a sweat and ran into their bedroom: "Please scratch my back!" turning his back to her. His wife, only half-awake, could not grasp what he wanted and began to stroke his back. For this he hit her with his left elbow knocking the poor woman almost unconscious. Running around the other rooms and the kitchen and unable to find any rough object to scratch against, Sychikhin went out on to the staircase of the apartment block, where the neighbours' daughter was kissing and scratching with her nails behind the ear of a spotty-faced youth.

"Hey you, buzz off!" Sychikhin barked, and the lad made off as if blown by the wind. "Nightbirds!"

"Come on now," Having rolled up his shirt and turned his back to the girl. "Here, scratch me!"

The fifteen-year-old Lena, wiping away her tears and smearing the mascara all over her face, clawed at Sychikhin's enormous back with her small painted fingernails. His voice took on a kinder note.

"It's nothing. Stop sniveling!" he comforted the girl. "Your boyfriend will come back. If he's keen on you he'll come back for sure. Or you'll find somebody else. How old are you?"

"Fifteen," Lena sobbed.

"You should be thinking about your studies. You doing well at school?"

Lena shook her head and blushed. This morning she'd got only a passing mark in geography.

True Woman

First Valezhnikov made a play for her but she turned him down because of his bandy legs.

Sayapin who, in contrast, had perfectly straight legs, thought that he might succeed. But he got nowhere either. With him it was ears. Sayapin's enormous jug ears played their unseemly role and he went away empty-handed.

Then Rakitsky, having studied the defects of Sayapin and Valezhnikov suddenly appeared on the horizon, took to dropping in and proved a smart operator. But he too had his flaws. First the bald spot on the back of his head that he couldn't quite comb over, and then all this overwork at the factory made him irritable and tired. So he went away for a while, to calm down and recover his strength.

Kazyulin. The handsome Kazyulin almost made it, assisted by Rakitsky's confusion. He had already reached the kissing stage, but at the last moment she began to think out loud:

"I am kissing Kazyulin!" And thus voiced, the words made the notion seem repellent. So she said, "Go away!"

"But why! Why!" said the baffled Kazyulin.

"Please go away," she said, pointing to the door.

Kazyulin burst into tears and ran down the stairs. His weeping could be heard in the street. But after a few minutes, from that very same street could be heard guffaws. This from Valezhnikov (remember him?) who had found out, or rather, guessed the reason for Kazyulin's misfortune and went running through the night streets pounding the pavement with his bandy legs, rejoicing that he was not the one suffering at that moment.

His laughter woke Sayapin next door who was sleeping on his side, one big ear squashed into the pillow. First he thought that it must be the laughter of success. But then he thought, "What sort of bloody success would have Valezhnikov guffawing in the street?" He looked out the window and saw both Valezhnikov and the receding Kazyulin. Realizing that there wasn't a moment to lose he pulled a cap over his ears to stop them flapping, dressed and ran to her flat. How fortunate that he lives next door. He burst into the main entrance like a whirlwind, and rang the doorbell. She didn't open it.

"What's going on? What's going on?" Sayapin was agitated. "Maybe Rakitsky's got rid of his bold spot and his situation at work has improved. And he's in there with her now!" He rang the bell again.

She peered through the peephole, hoping to see... You're thinking Rakitsky? Valezhnikov! You're dead right, that same Valezhnikov who at this moment is charging through the night streets on his bandy legs, the fool. (Later of course he will know what was in store for him. That he's missed his chance. She regrets it, but that comes later. Meanwhile he's belting through the dark cobbled streets on his bandy legs, cackling, and afraid of losing sight of the weeping Kazyulin.)

So here she is looking through the peephole at Sayapin with his jug ears crammed into his bonnet.

"Well," she thought, "Sayapin in his cap doesn't look too bad generally speaking." And she sensed a slight stab in her feminine heart.

"Who's there?" she called through the door, on purpose, as if she couldn't actually see through the peephole, "Is this Rakitsky?"

"Rakitsky's got a blotch on his head, and he's always in trouble at work," Sayapin called out and immediately regretted it. "I shouldn't have said that about him. I'll be in for it when I take my cap off."

He went in, took his coat off and began to talk more positively about Rakitsky. But only about his difficulties at work.

Meanwhile a man with a tired face was trudging towards this much-desired residence. He began to climb the stairs to the flat. His heavy steps and the sorrowful wrinkles on his face spoke of an overburdened and unsatisfactory working life. The well-combed hair on his head suggested a man who took pride in his appearance. The bouquet in his hands showed that he intended a rendezvous. Groaning, he reached the door, pressed the bell and thought dozily about how he would soon be sitting beside her and telling her all about his diabolically overburdened working life...

She didn't manage to get Sayapin's cap off until they got to bed. She realized that she was burning her boats, and tried not to look at those enormous ears flapping from time to time across her cheeks, and tried not to hear the endless ringing of the doorbell.

At such moments she would think about Rakitsky and his terrible working life. Or about Valezhnikov who at that moment was racing away from the night town towards the hills, his feet treading the valleys and clefts.

Eventually she married Kazyulin. A child appeared, whose ears had to be constantly hidden in a cap. If Kazyulin was on the scene he would grumble and she would weep.

Sayapin would sometimes observe these family outings from behind a tree: her, Kazyulin, and the boy with his ears wrapped up under a cap.

Rakitsky died of overwork.

But Valezhnikov went off to the mountains and wrote letters. After this she would often dream that she and Valezhnikov were climbing Mont Blanc, plodding upwards and laughing among the silence of the snows.

Lovely Lolita

Oh, what a marvelous wife Lolita is to Sebastian. That tiny miraculous Lolita, quiet and inconspicuous like a little mouse. As if a tiny living bundle is hiding behind the chest of drawers. And only those black eyes look playfully and tenderly from under her forelocks, to Sebastian's joy. He is contented with his wife. Look how he waddles around the house, arms open wide, searching, seeking through all the rooms, then around the kitchen.

"Lolita!" The weary Sebastian is looking for his wife. And she feels for him. Ready, steady, jump! Straight into Sebastian's arms. So warm that little soft bundle. She snuggles up to his chest, radiating love and tenderness. Sebastian puts his arms around her, kisses her, whispering in her ear. And she, Lolita shakes her forelocks in reply.

Sebastian knows that should he fall ill, suffer any

ailment, he would be tucked up into bed with his living bundle on his chest, his little mouse. And those same eyes trustfully gleaming black under her fringe will devotedly monitor the breathing, the pulse-rate of the groaning Sebastian. Then the return to well-being, and the love and joy renewed.

Now look at Lolita busying herself at the stove. Then with the washing, her hands rapidly working. And then she's not there. Where has she gone? On the verandah. Where, oh where are you? Quickly, quickly and there she is, straight into Sebastian's arms. What a darling housewife...

Sebastian overcomes his life's difficulties with love in his heart. Here he's lashing his bony old nag across a ploughed field. Now he's soaking in the rain trying to save the hay. Finally, having mastered the elements, he can lean back and rest.

Certainly that fat cook on the threshing floor can never replace Lolita. How can she be a substitute for that dark-eyed one who at a leap will smother him with kisses. Absolutely not, of course. How could that be with the cook? With all that weight. Right on the threshing floor. After the rain. As if you've been thumped by one of those heavy sacks at loading time. When two of the lads... with all their might... throw it, and you turn away. So that's how it is here. How she lands on you in the hayloft with all her body, knocking the breath out of you. Sebastian is exhausted in one go.

But then it's doubly joyful to return to Lolita, for her to jump into his arms as she flies down the corridor clasping Sebastian's thick-set neck with her supple arms. Lips, those luscious lips!

You see, it's quite a different matter.

The war did not pass by Sebastian's house. No, having waved goodbye to his loved one he shouldered his rifle and joined up with his column.

"I'll be back!"

And why not? Of course he'll return. Why wouldn't he? The whole column would return if each of them had a Lolita to come home to. But not everyone in the column has such a Lolita.

"I'll be back!"

Yes, Sebastian will come back home to Lolita.

Now can you really compare her with your long-legged high-cheek-boned town women? Those that flood the liberated towns after a battle. Her high heels clatter like hooves. Coarse bags of bones like Sebastian's old nag. When you carry this sort to the bed, it's like carrying a stepladder. You knock against the furniture, the lamp, and even the chandelier. With this one you will not whisper: "My little mouse" or "little bundle". For sure you will send flying either a vase or a bookshelf as you flop on to the bed with this carthorse. Sebastian sighs, scratching his injured spine. He rubs his bruised elbow. The only thing you get from these encounters is injuries and bruises. This is not Lolita. Oh no!

This is when he'd be pleased if his commanding officer would appear and send him on a mission. Sebastian surfaces with difficulty, rolls off this carthorse also with difficulty. Everything aches. His thoughts are muddled. It's all tottering. But he still has to go on. He must speak, obey, salute in the field. If he disobeys, then he can say goodbye to Lolita, the town mare, and even that distant fat cook on the threshing floor...

Run. Run. This is how it goes in war, you've got to keep on the move. So that's what Sebastian does. You shelter in any hole. And what joy, there's snow! Where better to dig in, provided the enemy hasn't got you in his sights. You crawl into a burrow. Good if there isn't a she-fox there. So what if there is? Well then... That's what Sebastian's thinking. "What then?" What won't you do to outwit a wriggling red-coated creature so it doesn't bite or twist, but lies peacefully. You caress it, scratch behind its ears, spin it long yarns. And there's still no guarantee that this lithe red traitor will be content to lie still and not jump, God forbid, into the snowy field, landing Sebastian into the hands of the watchful enemy. She'll pretend contentment and then how she'll jump. You better keep well away from these vixens.

But there aren't any women worse than those serving on the enemy's side. With them no tenderness or persuasion ever helps. Scratch behind the ear, or not, spin your long yarns... Useless! She will hiss, bare her teeth. Hurl obscenities at you. And they stink of petrol. To the left the mortar crew is working. Above, low-flying aircraft. And on the right a machine gun emplacement. Give them a smack in the gob, twist their arm behind their back as you trip them up. Get away out of the searchlight's range in your bullet-proof jacket. Yes and make sure she hasn't grabbed your holster. And God forbid she hasn't got as far as the grenade pins.

This is when Sebastian really remembers Lolita. That tender bundle. Oh wouldn't it be great if he could carry her with him as he breaks out of the encirclement. In his kitbag until the battle was over. And when it's over you open up and... There she is! There are those black eyes under the forelocks. Those soft arms. Well let's get on with it. Come on my lovely beauty! A leap and she's on your neck. Not one of those over-painted army wenches, peddling petty goods, who undresses you and runs off with your clothes, but Lolita; not the counter-spy who gets into your documents as she sighs erotically in your ear, but she's not Lolita, that most real Lolita, and who is for sure not any sort of nursing sister.

About the nursing sisters you simply wouldn't wish to remember. These nurses, you can't really call them women at all. Just as you make a narrow escape from an encirclement and drag yourself with enormous effort to the dressing station, this nurse, this blonde bitch may seem at first glance to be a Lolita. So tender and sensitive. "Be brave, my love, be brave..." Then in a moment she's with another casualty. And again, "Be brave, be brave..."

She's circling around, teasing the wounded. And at the slightest provocation she yells and calls for the chief surgeon.

One colonel (I don't quite remember his name) being discharged from the station said literally the following:

"If I ever again... One more time... That bloody bitch! (Talking about a nurse). Just once more..." He paused at a loss for words and lit up, adding: "When we went into battle, and right and left my mates were dropping dead..." He could say no more, sighed heavily and set off for the post office.

Artist Ruben Apresian

(See his pictures on the front and back covers)

By the early 1990s, Ruben Apresian was already a master of rich and powerful color compositions. However, recognizable forms of life were increasingly turning in his art into abstract forms. Obviously he was trying to express something of enormous importance to him rather than just tell more stories, imitating apparent reality. He strived to express his feelings directly and forcefully, bypassing nature, subject, and mimetic resemblance.

Ruben Apresian was born in 1963 in Moscow into a family of artists. In 1983 he enrolled in the Yerevan Art School, the department of woodcarving. But a year later he returned to Moscow and joined the studio of Iosif Gurvich, a follower of Cezanne, where he spent five years. At the same time he worked independently, took part in many professional art exhibitions, and frequently visited Armenia, the land of his ancestors.

Since 1984, Apresian has traveled extensively in Europe and displayed his work in more than fifty one-man shows and group exhibitions in Russia, Austria, and Germany.

In the last five years he regularly exhibits in the best exhibition halls of Moscow and St Petersburg.

Ruben Apresian's pictures are owned by the Tretyakov Art Gallery and Museum of Oriental Arts in Moscow, the Russian Museum in St Petersburg, Museum of the Mechitharist

Congregation in Vienna, Volksbank and Trossingen Stadtshaus collections in Germany, and by private collectors in Russia, Austria, Germany, the United States and South Korea.

"Ruben Apresian's art is inseparable from the entire evolutionary history of painting culture of the present and last century. His art possesses a certain linear inevitability combined with vibrant imagery where future meets the past, creating an inimitable phenomenon of his artistic perception of the world. Apresian's visual sensibilities are shaped by images taken from reality, thus bringing his own intuitive changefulness, breakthroughs and illuminations closer to the stylistics of the times. He manages to cross-connect artistic languages and find new strategic codes for his painting technologies. His creative approach never loses its relevance, expressing the unity of the apparent and the hidden, of the natural and born of the human intellect."

art critic Vitaly Patsukov

"Ruben Apresyan's art brings to mind the music of Beethoven, Brahms and Wagner, and also Alpine landscapes and the 18th century baroque architecture.

He is increasingly fascinated with triangles, ovals, zigzags and rectangles, which are more meaningful to him than the ideologies and passions of the collectivized humankind. The simplest visual reality and a quiet observation of this reality are more important to him than any ideas, values, and politics of our day and age."

art critic Alexander Yakimovich

GLAS BACK LIST

Asar EPPEL, *The Grassy Street*,
stories set in a Moscow suburb in the 1940s
Boris SLUTSKY, *Things That Happened*,
poetry & biography of a major poet
THE PORTABLE PLATONOV,
for the centenary of Russia's greatest writer
Leonid LATYNIN, *The Face-Maker and the Muse*,
a novel-parable
Irina MURAVYOVA, *The Nomadic Soul*,
a novel about a modern-day Anna Karenina
Anatoly MARIENGOF, *A Novel Without Lies*,
the turbulent life of a great poet against the
flamboyant background of Bohemian Moscow
Alexander GENIS, *Red Bread*,
Russian and American civilizations compared
Larissa MILLER, *Dim and Distant Days*,
childhood in postwar Moscow recounted with
sober tenderness and insight
Peter ALESHKOVSKY, *Skunk: A Life,*
Bildungsroman set in the Russian countryside
Ludmila ULITSKAYA, *Sonechka*,
a novel about a persevering woman
Andrei VOLOS, *Hurramabad*,
civil war in Tajikistan and fleeing Russians
Lev RUBINSTEIN, *Here I Am*, humorous-
philosophical performance poems and essays
Andrei SERGEEV, *Stamp Album*, **a collection of**
people, things, relationships and words
Valery RONSHIN, *Living a Life, Totally Absurd Tales*
Alexander SELIN, *The New Romantic,*
modern parables

GLAS BACK LIST

COLLECTIONS

REVOLUTION, the 1920s versus the 1980s
SOVIET GROTESQUE, young people's rebellion
against the establishment
WOMEN'S VIEW,
Russian woman bloodied but unbowed
LOVE AND FEAR, the two strongest emotions
dominating Russian life
BULGAKOV & MANDELSTAM,
earlier autobiographical stories
JEWS & STRANGERS,
what it means to be a Jew in Russia
BOOKER WINNERS & OTHERS
LOVE RUSSIAN STYLE, Russia tries decadence
THE SCARED GENERATION,
the grim background of today's ruling class
BOOKER WINNERS & OTHERS-II
CAPTIVES, victors turn out to be captives on
conquered territory
FROM THREE WORLDS, new Ukrainian writing
A WILL & A WAY, new women's writing
BEYOND THE LOOKING-GLAS,
Russian grotesque revisited
CHILDHOOD, the child is father to the man
NINE of Russia's Foremost Women Writers,
an anthology

BOOKS ABOUT RUSSIA

A.J.PERRY, *12 Stories of Russia: a Novel I guess,*
one American's adventures in today's Russia